I Want Your Body,
CANDY STARR

I Want Your Body, CANDY STARR

TOM KEMPINSKI

iUniverse LLC
Bloomington

I Want Your Body, Candy Starr

iUniverse books may be ordered through booksellers or by contacting:

iUniverse LLC
1663 Liberty Drive
Bloomington, IN 47403
www.iuniverse.com
1-800-Authors (1-800-288-4677)

ISBN: 978-1-4917-0950-4 (sc)
ISBN: 978-1-4917-0951-1 (e)

Library of Congress Control Number: 2013917553

Printed in the United States of America

iUniverse rev. date: 09/24/2013

Chapter One

I have this problem. I want to fuck Candy Starr.

Not Candy J. Starr, the stripper who changed her name from Annie Cranshaw to enhance her reputation and got taken to court and lost, thank God, I mean the <u>real</u> Candy Starr, the one who took the other one to court, the great movie star and the most glamourous woman in the whole wide world, <u>that</u> Candy Starr.

Now don't all start rushing around screaming and throwing your hands in the air and banging your heads against walls and foaming at the mouth and yelling "Women's Liberation" and "Male Chauvinist Pig" and writing to your senator and all that stuff, please. You have to grasp that I was born and raised in a part of New York where that type of thing don't go down so big, so I wasn't exposed to it much at all, really. Not that I am a male chauvinist either. Not at all. On the contrary. I treat women as my equals and I believe they are my equals and should be treated as such by society, and when I make love and have sexual intercourse and that kind of thing, I don't at all insist that I take a dominant role and lie on top, not always anyway and then go and tell my friends what kind of a lay she was, and all that.

But.

I do want to fuck Miss Starr, and all the liberated stuff only came to my attention after I got this fucking idea into my head anyway and it's very deeply ingrained in my psyche, and I don't honestly know if I can shift it and I don't even know if I want to. But I do know that I want that one thing very badly, and that's my problem.

Now I think I should explain in a little more detail what I mean when I say that I want to know Miss Starr in the biblical sense. See, I don't mean I just dream about fucking Candy Starr, though of course I do that too. I mean that I actually, physically, concretely, really want to fuck her. I don't just say I want to, but don't really want to. I actually do want to. In other words to put it another way. I really, honestly have the desire to be with her in the same room at the same time, and then start something. I mean like really, like you do it with your wife or your girl or your fella. You know, actually doing it.

O.K. So you may well say, "Big deal, he wants to fuck Candy Starr, everybody wants to fuck Candy Starr, so what's new?" But there you already reveal that you haven't understood me. See, the kind of man or woman who says, "I want to fuck Candy Starr" and then turns back to stir the pasta or fix the car or add up another column of figures does not in my opinion really want to do what I want to do. What that kind of person is really saying is "I envy the person who is fucking Candy Starr", or, "I would like to be in a position where I could fuck Candy Starr", but they're not saying that they themselves, as they are now, at that time, in their present position, want to fuck Candy Starr and they're gonna do it.

And I am.

And this is where the problem begins. Because I don't know Miss Starr, and she lives in California and I live in New York, and numerous other things, which is what this story is all about.

It all really started at the fan-club.

I joined my local Candy Starr fan-club a few years ago, and I really used to enjoy going. We used to meet every second Thursday of the month and we used to have a really great time. The committee used to get the room all fixed up with pictures of Miss Starr and of course we had posters of her films, and the committee, via the national organisation, had contacts with the various studios and film companies so they could procure stills from different scenes from her films and pictures of her relaxing between shots, or talking to her co-star or director, and they use to stick 'em up all over the walls, so that when members arrived, they walked into a situation where their favourite was just staring at them from every corner of the room. Then some nights we'd see a film of Miss Starr, or there'd be a discussion about her acting or about the critics, and we'd discuss what the likely problem was of a particular critic who's just given her a pasting, and all that sort of thing. For instance, there was a guy who said he had some training in psychology, and he'd analyse a particular criticism and show, for instance, that this critic had a mother fixation, or that he was a latent homosexual, or that he was worried about the size of his prick and that would make us feel really good, because we used to get very upset if Miss Starr received a bad review. And in fact the committee used to send her a letter on behalf of the club, telling her not to be upset

3

about the many bad reviews, and that we all thought she was terrific, and that we believed she ranked amongst the best screen actresses of the present day, and that kind of thing.

Then the committee used to organise raffles with a picture of Miss Starr or tickets to one of her movies as a prize and one of the members also used to invent cross-word puzzles exclusively about Miss Starr and her career. Of course some of the time at the club used to be taken up with collecting subscriptions and finance reports, which used to bore me somewhat, although some of the members used to like that side of it also. Also, I made a few friends and acquaintances there, so really it was a pretty good deal all round.

Then one day I flipped. I don't mean that I freaked out completely and thought I was Napoleon, but I definitely flipped, which is why I'm so sure about the difference between me and all the other people who say they want to fuck Miss Starr, and I'll show you what I mean.

What happened was this.

The chairman for that month was just announcing about the summer picnic we always had every year, and how everyone should get their tickets early because there was only limited accommodation on the bus, and not to forget rain-coats, and that members could each bring one non-member if there was still room on the coach, and stuff like that and I wasn't really listening because I'd heard it all, and I was just looking round the room at the posters and at the walls and at the members.

Now if you aren't a member of a Candy Starr fan-club some place, you have to understand that there are all kinds of people go to this type of a club. I mean ordinary people go there of course, married people and that sort, but you get some weird people too, naturally. Not a lot, of course. At least not in our club, but you do get some. I mean for a start, you get women who dress up to look like Candy Starr. Now I mean these women just don't look like Miss Starr at all. Some of them are very fat and some are tall and skinny and some are very small. And they don't look like her in the face either. Not just a little not like her. They don't look like her at all one little bit. I mean to be honest, some of these stupid women are extremely ugly people. But they still try to look like her by doing their hair like her or their eyes and that sort of thing. But they still don't look like her. They look like very ugly people with their hair <u>trying</u> to look like Miss Starr, but who definitely don't.

So I was just looking round, like I said, and suddenly I was looking at this woman, who I'd seen in the club for a long time. She was definitely a regular, and she looked like a heap of shit with a Candy Starr hair style. I mean honestly, I'm not being unkind or unsympathetic or anything like that, but this woman was really painful to look at. She must have weighed around eight-hundred pounds, she had on a short skirt which showed her thighs, which looked like two dead whales, she was showing her breasts, which looked like two whales' sick parents, and she was balancing her gut on her legs and it must have reached almost to her knees. And her face was pimply and quite red and looked very pushed in, as if it was being pulled back to fill a cavity in her skull. But her hair was cut like Candy Starr's.

And I stood up and shouted out, "This is all bull-shit."

Now the chairman was a guy called Johansen, who was a salesman of electrical equipment of some kind, and he was very amazed at what I said, because he had been selling us the bullshit along with the rest of the committee for quite a few years, and he didn't like being told it was bullshit, and it upset him very much.

So he said, "Did you want to say something, Mr Andretti?", and I said that I did.

"Yeah. I want to say that this whole thing is a lot of horse-shit."

Well you can imagine that this little exchange, and particularly my side of it, caused quite a sensation amongst the other members. I imagine they'd never had anything like this happen before, although they might have because I wasn't a founder-member of the club, and they were very embarrassed by the whole thing so far, although that wasn't the end of it. I guess they were surprised and sort of thrown off their balance like once I was driving with this guy next to me, suddenly he turns round and says, "Joe, can you pull over for a minute, I don't feel too good". Now immediately in that situation you get thrown off balance and your mind starts to imagine all kinds of things about the guy collapsing from a heart attack and rushing through the traffic taking the guy to hospital and that you don't know where the nearest hospital is and you remember some film, may be a comedy, where the husband is taking his wife to have the baby, and he asks the way to the hospital, but the guy he asks is deaf or Chinese or something, and it makes you laugh a lot, but not when it's you trying to find the hospital because your buddy has just collapsed right next to you.

And you get this mixture of feeling scared and unreal even though the whole thing is very real, because you've been just driving along, and maybe this is a regular thing going out with this guy, and you're just watching the road and thinking about something you read in the newspapers maybe about an earthquake in Turkey, and suddenly this smooth situation is completely blown away when the guy asks you to pull over in that quiet, panicky sort of voice.

And I guess that's how the other club-members mush have felt, because they're just sitting there hearing all this bull-shit about the picnic which they all know, and which is how they like the situation to be, and how it's always been, and as if from nothing this man who they think they all know about, stands up and says it's all bull-shit.

And suddenly I'm looking at the faces of about thirty people from the neighbourhood, because they've all turned around to look at me, except the Miss Spotty Red Face with the two dead whales and the parents of the two whales 'cos she's too fat to turn her head.

So the chairman continues with his relax-this-is-all-perfectly-normal-folks act and says, "O.K. Joe, this is the way we usually arrange the picnic, but if you've got some suggestions then we'd be glad to hear 'em."

Now he knows I ain't talking about the god-damn picnic, though he probably doesn't know fully what I <u>am</u> talking about, but he can tell from my voice and the emotion that's coming through that I'm not talking about that, but he's trying to keep things calm, so he asks me for suggestions about the frigging picnic.

To which I say, "I ain't got no suggestions about the picnic."

To which he says, "You haven't?"

To which I say, "No."

To which he says, "Well Joe, the picnic is the item on the agenda which is being discussed right now."

To which I reply, "You know god-damn well I ain't talking about the fucking picnic."

Which he does. And so does everybody else.

Well that's too much for Johnny Futelli.

Johnny Futelli works for the Docks Board in quite a respectable position, but he used to be a docker, and he's built along the lines of Rocky Marciano. which he will often tell you. Now Futelli is this kind of man; he goes out every night to some bar, maybe alone or with a friend, and when he's had a few beers, he looks around for someone he can attack. And he always finds someone, and then he attacks them. And he doesn't always attack smaller men than him. Quite often he attacks bigger men than him, and he usually puts them away too. And when he can't, he waits for 'em outside the place and then puts them away with a bottle or an iron bar.

Now these kind of people don't attack someone because they're drunk. They get drunk to release their morality which then allows them to do what they want, which is to attack people. Because out of their development as people they have simply become violent.

But.

With women and even with his wife. Johnny behaved in a very gentlemanly way. He never swore in front of a woman, though he'd be cuntassfuckshit with you all day, when it came to women, he'd treat them like each one was the Virgin Mary with the Pope listening in on the extension.

So Futelli gets to his feet and looks over at me. His face has his favourite 'I-am-controlling-my-anger-with-difficulty-but . . . .' expression on, before he attacks you with self-righteous fury for the injury you have done him, which he provoked in the first place anyway.

"Would you be kind enough to moderate your language Andretti," he says.

You see? You see what I mean? 'Moderate'. Would I moderate my language? Normally he'd say to you, "Shut your ass, or I'll shove a broom handle up it", or "Quit yapping, or I'll stuff four pricks down your throat." And now the man, who is very <u>unmoderate</u> when he's away from women, is asking me, asking me, right, to be moderate. So his whole spiel was just so much more bull, and I was just going to tell him so, even though he was very violent, and successfully so, when the chairman interrupts me because he senses also that Futelli is about to launch into his flying Superman act all over his nice, tidy Candy Starr fan-club.

"That's alright, Mr Futelli", he says, "let's be democratic about this and let Joe have his say."

Now one of the many things I have noticed on my journey through this vale of tears like the priest used to say is that whenever someone wants to put himself in the right he poses as a democrat. This word democracy is like a perfume. Whenever people want to smell real nice to other people they put on a little democracy so that everyone will love them and say what a deeply principled person and regular guy they are, and then vote for them or work for them for nothing or give them ten bucks and join their organisation. As far as I can see everyone's a democrat, and the fascists who stuffed Jews into the gas-chambers probably claimed they were only carrying out their democratic right to obey orders and likewise that bastard in Bosnia probably. And what made it worse, everyone knew that this chairman was a real pusher and that all he wanted was to get to be chairman of the Candy Starr fan-clubs nation-wide, and meet the president and get the congressional medal of honour and a million bucks a day tax—free and have the president's wife lick his dick on a regular basis.

So his cute little speech only served to make me more sick of the whole outfit, because to be frank with you, when they say 'he's snapped' that's exactly what happened to me at the moment I saw the two dead whales and the parents of the two whales, and I was just about ready to take the piece that snapped off and shove it down Futelli's ear, and the rest of the club members' ears also.

So I looks over at Futelli and then I throw my little anti-Candy Starr fan-club neutron bomb, which destroys Candy Starr fan-clubs and their phoney members but leaves Candy Starr intact.

"Look", I says, "I wasn't talking about the picnic and you all know it. I was talking about this whole outfit. I was talking about this whole god-damn club and about all of you including Futelli and that's what is horse-shit around here. Because what is going on around here is not what it appears. What is going on here is that all of you women want to be Candy Starr and you want her money and her appearance and her fame and you want to be fucked like her and meet the men she meets instead of the boring creeps you normally associate with, and you think by coming here you'll get just a sniff of the real action and that stops you going crazy and grabbing a rifle and shooting at people from the United Nation's building, because you all have boring, meaningless lives and you know that it'll never be any different and playing at being Miss Starr is the only thing that's holding you together, and the men only come here for one reason also," and I was talking real fast now, because I knew that the little neutrons had almost found their targets, and that when they did, considerable disorder would ensue, "which is because you want to fuck Candy and you know you can't so you cover up with a lot of horse-shit about her acting and discussing her artistic attributes when all you're doing is thinking about her cunt into which you want to insert the largest length of dick you can manage, including sticking a dildo on the end because you're so god-damn scared you don't match up," and out of the corner of my eye I can see Futelli coming for me. He's not moving that fast, because he's trying to avoid breaking his wife's legs next to him as he passes her along the row, and also the legs of the woman sitting next to her, who is looking at me with her mouth so wide I can see the gold fillings on her back teeth. And I'm moving along my row away from the direction of Futelli not caring about anyone's legs, and the chairman is shouting for silence, but when the anti-Candy Starr fan-club neutron bomb has exploded, shouting is simply a waste of time, because you're setting off a chain reaction which goes deep to the roots of things and is deaf to the protests of politeness. And I just get a flash of everyone else gawping, and then someone hits me on the nose from the other side from Futelli, where I'm not looking.

I am not a violent man. Not that I'm a conscientious objector or a peacenik or would have gone on demonstrations against the war in the Gulf or Vietnam or nothing like that, though I don't support war much, but to me, being against violence is like being against rats. Nobody likes 'em, but nobody knows where they come from or how to get rid of them. So you just try to avoid 'em. And that's my position on violence.

Let me give you another example about violence over and above the example of Futelli. I once knew this guy who was an actor, or he'd become an actor. I met him when I used to take out this girl who used to make costumes for one of the off-Broadway theatres and her friend was a model and one of this model's fellas was this man who had become an actor. Because before he was an actor he was something of a small-time hood. Not that he was in the Family or anything like that as far as I know, but he'd been in a hospital for the criminally insane for cutting someone's arm off with a hack-saw and he'd been offered another contract on a man in Belgium who was a business rival of the man who offered the contract, though I don't think he took up the offer because by that time he'd decided to divert his violence into the rather more creative pastime of acting, which he had got into when one of the modern generation of directors was making a gangster movie and wanted someone who could do what he called live the part.

Now this actor, who I will call Chris to protect the innocent, namely myself, had a very unhappy childhood which I know is a very corny thing to say but about this Chris it is true as you will see by the following example. On Sundays, Chris's father, who was a policeman, used to put him under the kitchen table if, for instance, this Chris had spoken out of turn or if the father was just feeling a little out of sorts, and he'd push the kid's plate under there with him and say, "Eat that, dog. You're a dog. Eat where the dogs eat," and he'd kick him every so often which is presumably how he treated dogs. And he'd keep the kid there all day sometimes and every so often during the day when he was passing he'd give his son a kick or a dig with a chair leg that was standing by handy.

Now I'm no expert on psychology and I've only read one book about it which was a book about positive thinking which someone gave me once when I was feeling a bit low and I wanted to change my job, but you don't need to be no Einstein to know that that kind of treatment of a kid is not going to make for a positive outlook on life in general. So this Chris took to sawing people's limbs off with a hack-saw blade for cash and now you can see why.

Also, as this Chris grew up it turned out that he had an exceptionally long prick. He could grab hold of it with his hand and enough would still be showing for him to wave it round in a circle. And I mean without an erection. So just to prove he wasn't a dog and was better than his father, he developed this habit of taking out his prick in public and waving it around or maybe he's be in a bar and when someone came to serve him he'd put the prick on the bar and say "Give me a Martini, I'll stir it myself with this", or "Just a plate and some mustard please," and of course there'd usually be some poor unknowing jerk there who'd say, "Hey, do you mind fella, we've all got one so could you put it away where it lives please," and then Chris used to smash the guy to pieces for keeping him under the table for so long.

Well I'm not the Chris/ Futelli type.

But.

When I get hurt physically I do go into a great rage. It's not that I turn around and weigh up the offender and then feint with a left and finish him off with a right hook to the exact place on the jaw where it joins the skull, which is where they used to say the nerve is which knocks you out, (which is completely wrong, but anyway.) When I get hurt, I just go into a completely unscientific rage.

So when I get this blow on the nose I turn round and for an instant see the face of Jim Green who is a waiter in a restaurant and weighs about seventeen pounds wet and wears glasses and I punched him right on the forehead and twisted my wrist which became extremely painful.

By now the place is in a total chaos with all the Candy Starrs screaming and chairs falling to the ground and Futelli still getting nearer and who is now screaming, "You cunt, you cunt," for which he would later apologise publicly to the entire club, I heard.

So I made my escape climbing over chairs and Candy Starrs and ran out into the street and kept on running for a while because I realised that there are certain situations in which explanations will not be accepted by people and I'd just created one. So the club lost a membership fee but wouldn't worry because there are plenty more phonies where they came from.

Chapter Two

I was a few blocks away from the club and instinctively I thought I might as well go on a zig-zag, but almost immediately I realised that I'd never be going on a zig-zag or a huddle again. Now I'll have to explain this.

As I described earlier, we didn't just meet at the club once a month and talk. We engaged in numerous activities, some of which I have already mentioned and also it goes without saying that we'd go to the airport to greet Miss Starr if the committee found out she was on a visit to New York, and we had Miss Starr painting competitions and Miss Starr poetry competitions and Miss Starr song contests. Some of the poems were very good and we got one printed in the papers once. Also we were the most vociferous fans at Miss Starr's premieres where we stood outside the movie theatre screaming and clapping. And then there were the zig-zags and huddles.

A huddle is the following. Everyone at the club would vote for a particular movie theatre where one of Miss Starr's films was showing and then the whole club would go there and stand in a huddle outside. We didn't go there to see the movies on these occasions. We'd just stand outside looking at the pictures or 'still' as they call them from the film, and at the lady's name on the hoardings and at the whole outside of the theatre where it had anything to do with our favourite and we'd make an analysis of the whole coverage of Miss Starr undertaken by this particular theatre. We would then make a whole series of comparisons, for instance with the coverage given to other stars at this theatre, with the coverage given to Miss Starr at other theatres, with the coverage given to Miss Starr by this and other theatres of her previous films or with the previous coverage of this film at another theatre if this was the second showing of this particular film.

And so on.

And this work was not undertaken in a light-hearted or unscientific way. We used to measure the size of the photographs, and count the number of photographs in which Miss Starr appeared alone and the number in which she was shown with one or more other actors. We'd count the number of photographs in which Miss Starr was depicted in a bathing costume or with her dress half torn off, as compared to the photographs in which she wore an outfit which concealed her figure, and these would again be subdivided into those with a plunging neck-line and those without one, and so on. From this we could chart the degree to which the film companies were taking Miss Starr seriously as an actress. We also purchased a device with which we could, from across the street from the theatre, measure the size of her name above the title of the film and the size of her name compared to the size of her co-star's name.

In this way we amassed a large amount of data and all this data would be analysed and from it we would get all kinds of facts about Miss Starr's status in the eyes of the studio and the distributors and the movie houses and so on and if we didn't like the attitude of a particular movie theatre or movie company towards Miss Starr, we used to write to them or get together with other clubs and write a joint letter, or even send delegations to theatres or studios to press for our point of view which we always made sure was in line with what we understood was the aims and hopes of Miss Starr at that particular time in her career. For instance, if her co-star had the same billing as her and from our analysis of his career we felt that he didn't deserve it, we'd write about that. Or if a certain film was one of the increasing number of serious ones she was making and the theatre manager had selected for his publicity the only scene in the film where Miss Starr showed a significant amount of her body, and the selections from this one scene were out of all proportion to the importance of the scene in the actual film, we might consider this worthy of a small or medium-sized delegation depending on how serious we assessed the potential damage to Miss Starr's hopes for her future.

This was the purpose of the huddle.

Now since anti-bullshit is part of the weave of this book I cannot pass on without revealing to you the true nature of all this Sherlock Holmes type of research.

From the dropping of certain hints and phrases by club members, say on the side-walk after a club night or in the john at the wash stands and not least from my own observation of myself, it became clear to me over the years that the huddle also had certain unofficial functions over and above those stated in the rules of the club, where the huddle was now enshrined as a legitimate club activity. Firstly, members went on a huddle simply to look at Miss Starr's image. To look, to gaze, to gawp, to guzzle, to drool, to swallow, to suck, to inhale. And without that sense of embarrassment we felt if we stared at her pictures by ourselves at home. Because on a huddle you could spend long minutes devouring the stills without feeling you was a peeping-tom or that passers-by thought you were a pervert or a dirty old man or a lesbian of some kind. (Not that we didn't all stare at pictures of Miss Starr in the privacy of our homes anyway, but when you're doing it with someone else AND the club rules say it's legitimate, there is a great sense of release from guilt).

But the huddle had an even deeper hidden significance if you want my honest opinion. As we stood before the pictures of Miss Starr, measuring and comparing, counting and collating, we peered at her face and body searching minutely for the ravages of time. Oh yes! We weren't only counting inches, we was counting wrinkles, we weren't only comparing the size of photos, we were comparing the size of her breasts. Had the lid begun to droop over those magnificent eyes? Was that hip beginning to stick out a little and unbalance the perfect proportions of her legs? Was that an expression or were those lines starting to fall diagonally from the corners of that perfect mouth? Right in the middle of our cheerful duties we fearfully scanned the surface of those photographs for the tell-tale signs of age.

Of course at the club we happily and openly discussed the future progress of our dream-girl into middle and old-age. Some saw her as withdrawing suddenly into a mysterious retirement like Garbo, others spoke of her natural development into character roles providing her increasingly with the serious acting parts she craved and deserved, other spoke of marriage and a family and the fulfillment of the womanly role denied her by the pressures of stardom. But in our hearts we anxiously resisted the movement of time. We wanted her as she was when she first burst in on our lives and we wanted her so eternally. On one occasion we saw some pictures of Bardot which showed her drooping bosom and we turned our eyes from each other and stared guiltily at the floor.

And as we probed the pictures we adjusted the focus of our vision and looked at the reflections of ourselves in the protective sheets of glass, at the jacket we could no longer close over our belly, at the receding hair-line, at the fattening jaw. We were growing old together, the huddle and Miss Starr, but we fought back against it with an angry despair.

She was the measure of our lives, of the fleeting years of our fleeting youth. As long as she showed no signs of age, time stood still for us too.

That in my opinion was the real purpose of the huddle.

The zig-zag was different.

A zig-zag was a journey backwards and forwards across New York taking in every theatre showing a Candy Starr movie. (Somebody once raised the idea of a national zig-zag but no-one in our club had that kind of money). A zig-zag could start out from the club and be done by individuals or couples or by a group—in which instance it took on some of the features of a huddle—or you could do it in your own time say after work or late at night. The purpose here was to get an overall picture of Miss Starr's power in the entertainment life of the whole city and zig-zags were compared week by week and with last year's zig-zags and so on and so on and so on.

Of course zig-zags used to take on a pretty competitive aspect too as you can imagine. Club night someone reports on his zig-zag.

". . . . and then on to the Bronx by sub-way where I was able to catch a cab right outside the movie, straight over to Times Square . . . .", and how long it took, and alternative methods of transportation and how much it cost and how to do it in a blackout and how to do it after the nuclear holocaust and after a terrorist attack . . . . Oh yes. We had some real zig-zag freaks in the club. You know. Like the potential president of Standard Oil who climbs Everest and then has to do it again naked, climbing backwards without ropes and with a special machine which reduces the amount of oxygen and then you don't hear about him for a long time because he's become the first solo yachtsman across the universe, travelling on a five million year old papyrus reed and propelling himself by shear god-damn will-power.

You know. We're all doing it, ain't we? "I've found this new way . . .".

So now I've dropped the anti-Candy Starr fan-club neutron bomb and I'm standing next to two garbage cans and I know I will never go on another zig-zag or huddle. Not because I can't, as you can see, but because I have chosen a different road. From now on it's the real thing. No more substitutes. Fuck or bust. The only zig-zag I was going on was inside Miss Starr. And huddle too. Down with crisp-bread, long live bread, down with Soya beans, long live cows, down with Bush, long live democracy.

I took the subway home.

My room as you would expect is covered with pictures of Miss Starr. Walls, ceiling, floor. (On the floor I covered the pictures with industrial plastic). And when I say covered, I mean it. Every inch of that box is papered with her pictures and one window too. And I am in a continuous process of redecoration. As I procured new pictures I would remove ones that I had got tired of masturbating to or just got tired of and replace them with the latest of the greatest. When the landlord first saw it he was very insecure.

"So what's this?"

"This is pictures of Candy Starr."

"I can see that, Andretti, what it means?"

"It means the same as the shit-brown in the corridor and the piss-yellow in the bath-room. It's decoration."

"Not piss-yellow. Sungleam."

"Whatever."

"I'm not sure if I like this, Andretti. What it for? Keep you warm at night." And he laughed. As you know, owning property and collecting rent gives you certain rights one of which is to have a sense of humour without having one.

"What if the next tenant don't like it?"

"There won't be no next tenant, the house won't last that long because you never do no repairs, but if it does I swear on the grave of my second cousin twice removed Nelson Rockefeller that I will return the room to its former glory."

"You related to Rockefeller?"

"Only by blood."

"Then why you live in a crap place like this?"

"I want to experience the life of the poor and downtrodden so when one of my companies goes bust I know how miserable they'll feel."

"What companies you got?"

So I got to keep the pictures.

When I first put up the pictures, which took me several months to collect and stick on, I just stuck 'em up any old how. I just started in the top corner and worked my way around and down, cutting and pasting, so there was no pattern or organisation of the pictures. Then over the years I began to arrange and re-arrange the pictures in a variety of ways. First I put them in groups like all the bikini shots in one group, all the head shots in another group and the leggy ones in another group and so on. Then I grouped 'em according to films, which was very laborious and took a lot of research, then in chronological order starting at the door, and so on. So the room was constantly changing its appearance and since I couldn't change much else about it on my pay as a hospital porter, it kept things fresh and interesting.

So when I opened the door to my room you could say I was surrounded by Miss Starr though of course only by images of her.

Which brings me to masturbation.

Everyone in the club used to masturbate to pictures of Miss Starr. I knew that from talking to a few close associates over the years, usually over a drink after club night, and I was no exception. And I honestly don't think it shows any lack of respect unless you think jerking off is dirty, and in fact it's really a compliment if you think about it, because it means that at the very least you find the physical side of her attractive though Miss Starr meant a lot more than that to me of course.

Now quite a lot of writing and research about sex has come out in the last few years about people's habits and the female orgasm and stuff like that, but I've never seen a book about masturbation and I got the idea of a questionnaire about masturbation which would really go into the art and science of it and would prove a great help to young men by improving their technique and easing their fears about it and bringing even greater enjoyment to a whole lot of people, because I'd found that over the years I had learned a lot about how to get the best out of it and that it wasn't just a question of moving your hand up and down your prick and standing by with a tissue or running over to the wash stand at the last moment. And I don't see why if all them people with letters after their names can make themselves a fortune by writing books called 'A thousand ways to please your partner' and 'Good sex is giving sex' and go on the Oprah Winfrey Show to advertise, I can't get a little bit of the action also and this is the kind of thing I had in mind.

QUESTIONNAIRE ABOUT MASTURBATION

(All answers will be treated in the strictest confidence).
Please put a tick in the appropriate box and try to answer
all questions.

                                                          YES   NO

1)   Do you masturbate?

2)   Do you masturbate often?

3)   How often? (Write in once a week, three
     times a day, etc.)

4)   Do you enjoy it?

5)   Do you feel guilty about it?

6)   Why? (If not, ignore this question, but
     please try to be honest about it)

7)   Are you afraid your father will break down
     the door and catch you red-handed?

8)   Are you afraid your mother will call your
     father to break down the door?

9)   If your father caught you, do you think he
     would: a) beat the living daylights out of
     you; b) pretend he didn't care; c) show you
     how to do it better? (put a), b) or c), or write
     in any alternative

10) How does this fear affect your performance?
     (e.g. do you hurry over the thing or
     whatever. Please restrict your answer to
     twenty words)

11) How many times can you manage to come
     in one session, and at what time intervals?
     (Please try to be honest with this question
     also)

12) Where do you do all this? (Toilet, bed, field, Lincoln Centre?)

13) Do you have a sister?

14) Has she caught you?

15) Have you caught her?

16) What was the outcome of this? (Please restrict your answer to twenty words again on this particularly confidential reply.

Example:—"I caught my sister and she nearly jumped out of her skin, but said she was scratching herself but I knew. She has never admitted it, but has barred me from her family's house since I mentioned it again recently considering she's grown up now and has a family." This example is more than twenty words).

17) Where do you hide the books and magazines?

(And so on with a whole series of general questions, but then you get to the meat of the matter which is technique).

49) Do you use a lubricant? (Avoid brand names)

50) By how much does this improve your enjoyment? (10%, 20%, 50% etc.)

51) Which is better, the up stroke or the down stroke? Up . . . . Down . . . .

52) Do you twirl your fingers round the knob in a clockwise and anti-clockwise direction alternately like one of those old-fashioned orange-juice makers?

53) Did you know that if you tickled your balls and jerked off at the same time allowing one break in the rhythm after every two strokes that this works very well?

Etcetera.

And if I'm going to be totally honest with you, it wasn't so much a questionnaire that I thought of this whole thing for, but more as a list of my own experiences which I thought I could put into a book, and I thought I'd call it 'Masturbation Manual', which isn't bad, and I really thought I might make a few bucks out of if considering the universal interest in the subject-matter. And by the way, most of my technique had been learnt at the expense of Miss Starr though not all as you will see.

What is worrying me somewhat is that some of you may have gotten the impression that I'm some kind of St. Petersburg clerk in the Russia of the Czar who goes into his little office every day in a long black coat and then back home at night and never has any kind of life and wants to sleep a lot. This is not at all what I'm like. Completely apart from the club and Miss Starr (which puts me outside the clerk category anyway), I lead a full social and sexual life which means I take girls out for meals and to the movies, often to a Candy Starr film of course, and bring them home or go to their place and have intimate relations with them, and I've taken a girl on a holiday to Mexico and others to other places, so I'm no Ivan Ivanovitch.

But what I believe is interesting here and what has always surprised me and why I told you about the wall decoration and my masturbation, is how these girls react when they come into my room and see Miss Starr looking at them from all sides and down on their heads and up their skirts. Because they must know that the guys they go with jerk off and maybe the most they've seen is a copy of Playboy or Shoot or whatever lying around in their rooms, and here they come into a place that's plastered quite openly with eight million pictures of a woman who they know just destroys them from the physical point of view and with a man who is quite open about letting them see these things, and the amazing thing is the way most of these women more or less accept the whole thing, I mean like the room decoration and everything associated.

Of course, they all mention it more or less right away. (Except one who didn't say a word and left after a drink saying she wasn't that kind of a girl). But then they ask me about it and I tell them what it's all about and some get quite interested, some say I'm crazy or that I should grow up, but with the one exception we fuck in the normal way and I've had quite steady relationships with these girls and though they may rib me a little, I guess they treat me and Candy like some kind of a hobby like fishing or collection turtles. Maybe it's because she's just pictures and they're real, I don't know, but that's how it is.

The only person who gave me any real trouble about this was girl called Gail. Gail served hamburgers in a little red hat and she was what I call tight although she was also very sensitive and intelligent as you will see. She was short and had blonde dyed hair which was thick and curly and lacquered, and a beautiful round face with thick pouting lips and a straight small nose and her breasts were big and stuck right out but they hardly swayed at all when she walked, which could have been her bra but wasn't, because when I got there, they were very full and tight and hardly changed their shape when she was lying on her back. And her ass stuck out too and was very tight and her legs were rounded and very firm and so were her shoulders. And for all I know her cunt was tight too, but I never found out as you will also see.

This Gail was very sought after by men and I had to wait in line sort of, but my turn came, as it will if you want it to, and I asked her out. And she looked at me and her face said, "This is what I'm thinking and I know what you're thinking and I want you to know that I know, and I want you to know that I'm in agreement and we're both thinking the same and the answer is DICK/CUNT." So we had a drink together after work and went back to my picture library. And she looks at the pictures and asks me about 'em and I told her something of what I've already told you and she laughs a little but you could see from the way she stood next to some of the pictures and smiled and stuck her chest out that she wasn't brought down by Miss Starr's physique at all.

And quite soon with no fuss we're making it on the bed.

Now this Gail really enjoyed sexual intercourse with a man. I don't mean she was a good fuck, which I consider an insult, she was a woman who got pleasure from it, and when you have two people who feel like that, the excitement is enormous. So without going into a long description, because you've all been there, most of you, after half an hour I'm sitting on her chest with my knees on her shoulders pulling her head into my crotch with my prick in her mouth and she's giving herself a manual clit-fuck, and suddenly she tries to say something.

"Waip a minupe."

I thought she was just getting turned on, so I continued with the business in hand, or mouth, really.

But she turns her head sideways and slips my prick out of her mouth and says it again.

"Wait a minute will you?"

Now my prick was about three miles long and as hard as Scrooge's bargaining and I was half-way up the drive to the gates of heaven and I didn't want to wait a minute.

"What honey. What's wrong?"

"I want to ask you something."

"Later honey, I'll tell you later, anything, I promise, but later."

"I WANT TO KNOW WHAT YOU'RE THINKING."

And she pushed me and I was on my back with my prick pointing into Candy's left eye on the ceiling, and she gets up and starts to pace.

My dick is starting to die.

"What's the matter Gail?"

"I want to know what you're thinking."

"Well I'm not thinking about Cuba I can tell y . . . ."

"You're just using me to fuck her, aren't you?"

"Wha . . . . ?"

"That's why you had me lying on you eating my cunt, so that you could look up at her through my ass and pretend you were fucking her wasn't it?"

"Honey honestly . . . ." And I went over to her and tried to put my arms around her to convince her and she slapped me very hard.

"You fucking bastard, that's what you get girls up here for so you can use them to jerk off on and think about her."

And she started to cry and sat on the floor and just wept, and I was really surprised and upset because I really didn't do what she said but I couldn't convince her whatever I said.

"Don't tell me, you're all the fucking same."

And then it all came out. Her husband that was had, on the night of a particularly successful fuck, screamed out 'Judith' when he came and Judith was her very sexy friend and after that she could never have sex with him and they separated not long after and she thought I was doing the same sort of thing. And she got more and more upset and suddenly jumped up and tried to tear down Candy from the wall and I got angry and slapped her and then tried to apologise and comfort her and get her back to the bed, but the whole thing was a mess by now and she left and wouldn't even let me see her to a cab. I tried to date her again and she ate a hamburger with me but that was all, and I honestly think that the event with her husband had seriously undermined her personality and her self-confidence and I really felt sorry for the kid but, of course, I wasn't the man to set things right. I was now the Candy-man like her husband was the Judith-man.

But other than Gail, I really didn't have a lot of trouble about Candy and the pictures.

So this is how it all went on between me and masturbating and Candy and girls.

Chapter Three

When I got home from the club that night, I had an hour to kill because Loreen was coming over but of course she didn't know that I left early due to unforeseen circumstances. So I just lay down on the bed and looked up at the full length picture of Candy which I'd pasted right above, in which she'd wearing just enough, and I started to think, which that picture always made me do.

Now I know that there's not disputing taste as they say in the movie magazines and everyone has their own opinion and there's no right and wrong about opinions and all that, but I can prove to you that Miss Starr is the most beautiful woman in the world and this is why.

As I told you, Miss Starr was not the first lady to make me come through my own efforts and before her there was Raquel Welsh and Tonia 'Try Me' Angels and I need hardly tell you that they're both very good-looking women and of course there's been dozens of stars and models who are all beautiful and well-stacked and pretty and where you want to put your head between their thighs and the full business.

But.

Here's where Candy scores.

If you really study Candy you'll see that she has everything. And I don't mean in that corny sense of "Gee that Angelina Jolie (or whoever) sure has everything in the right place." I mean that Miss Starr has many sides to her appearance all present at the same time. For instance, look at her face, which I did there on the bed. Now no-one would deny that she has a very feminine face. She has beautiful large eyes with long lashes and a beautiful head of red hair and a pair or full sexually stimulating lips and she looks in every way a woman facially. But. There is also a strength there which is masculine. A strong nose, a firm jaw-line, a straight look. So right away you have two sides to her face which a lot of fine looking chicks don't have, as for instance Pamela Anderson. Now Anderson is a beautiful woman and a fine actress, but if you take her face, it's cute and sexy and child-like and fun but nowhere can you see anything masculine about it at all, so right away you see what I mean about Candy having lots of different things in her face at the same time. Or take Nicole Austin where again you have the sex side to the fore, with the baby thing and the need for protection, but nowhere the male side. Or take Candy again. You could have Candy in a movie play a duchess or a tramp, you could put her hair up and put a tiara on her head and diamond necklace and ear-rings and she's class, or you could put her on the streets with a skirt up around her ass and sling-back shoes and a blouse open down to her waist and you believe she does it for money and has been all her life. But you dress Julia Roberts like that and she's without a doubt one of the most beautiful women there's ever been, and she'd look like Rockefeller's wife at a fancy dress ball for low lifes, you just wouldn't believe she'd ask you for the two hundred bucks.

Then again you take Candy's body. Now Candy is not a big woman but you put her in a dominating part and she'll look ten feet tall or you give her the part of a ballerina and she's tiny like you could blow her away, and whatever you say about say Russell or Ekberg from the olden days, and Jesus Christ there you have two fantastic women, unbelievably good-looking and overpowering, but no way could you believe that they could do a pirouette without overbalancing. Or you take Candy's breasts (and I will and you can make a book on it). Now if you're what they call a tits man she has got a beautiful pair; enough to satisfy any tit fetishist around, but on the other hand if you're like a guy I once knew from our neighbourhood who works in a gas-station, he once saw me looking at the inside pages of Boobs and he says "I don't know how you can stand looking at those kind of dames, who wants a woman with two water melons sticking out of her front?" And Candy's bosoms would in no way seem distasteful to a guy like that who likes 'em small and neat.

And Candy's like that in every department; like if you like the thought of being crushed between two powerful muscular thighs, she fits the bill, but if you like slim legs, she has those, whereas Claudia Schiffer has only the slim thing to offer. And so on, whatever you care to mention.

And I was just lying there thinking these things over in my mind, which I had once given as a talk at the fan-club and which I also thought of writing in a book and making some dough out of like the manual manual, if you get my meaning, when there's a knock on the door and it's Loreen who comes in.

"Hi."

"Hi."

I've been taking Loreen out for about three months without too much hassle and she's a woman who would be an obvious target for the tit-fetishists that I mentioned earlier, though not for face-fetishists, and when she walks her hips move about two feet from side to side of the centre line to ensure that she's noticed and is never short of company.

"How was the club?"

"I left early."

"You left early! Why, what happened, they declared war?"

"I told 'em they could shove it 'cos it was all bull and they got upset so I left."

"You what!?"

"Yeah."

"What happened for Christ's sake?"

And you know I hadn't really thought about what had really happened 'cos on the subway I'd just gone over it in my mind and on the bed I'd been thinking about Candy and I really hadn't thought about what was at the root of any of it. So I sat up on the bed.

"I don't know really, I just got pissed off."

"You got pissed off with THIS?" And she swung her hand towards one of the walls.

"No, not with Candy, with the club."

"Why, did someone say something?"

"Not more than usual."

"So?"

"I don't know. Just a whole lot of little things that I've seen for a long time they just got to me, it's all so phoney.

"What?"

"Oh I don't know. All those dames trying to be like her and all the talk and never coming out with what it's really all about."

"That makes you a phoney too."

"That's right, I was for a long time, that's why I left."

"What are you going to do, you going to tear all this down?"

Should I keep it a secret from her? I could, but then somebody would probably find out while I was making the arrangements to see Candy and tell Loreen anyway, so I might as well get used to someone's attitude right away.

"No. I've decided to fuck Candy."

"What?"

"I'm going to fuck Candy."

"What are you talking about?"

I was getting nervy.

"What do you mean what am I talking about, I said I'm going to fuck Candy. You know, with my prick, you know, fuck, OK?"

"But you don't even know her."

"I didn't know anybody before I knew 'em did I? I didn't know you before I knew you, did I?"

"But you can't just fuck people like that."

"Why not, someone fucks her."

"Yeah but not you."

"You mean I'm not class enough."

"How do you know she'll agree?"

"You agree don't you? And you ain't the first."

"The fastest fuck in the West huh? 'I am the man who fucked Candy Starr'. Suddenly you're Mr Big."

Sometimes I hate cute women because when women get cute they start to know what's happening.

"I'm big enough for you anyhow."

"Joe you're crazy. I never thought you were crazy but now you are."

"What's crazy about it?"

"That's how crazy you are, you don't even know."

"Then tell me what's crazy about it if you're so frigging clever and then I will frigging know."

"Oh come on Joe."

"What come on?"

"She's got body-guards and everything."

"So maybe she fucks her body-guards and maybe I'll get a job as a body-guard, who knows, do you?."

"Oh for Christ's sake!"

But she couldn't really tell me why I couldn't fuck Miss Starr though she put up a lot of difficulties but I really couldn't see the problem. So in the end we went to bed, so she couldn't have thought I was that crazy, and we finished with me fucking her up the ass which is how she always wanted it, though I didn't rate it tops and in the morning when I got up to go to the john someone had locked the door of my room from the outside.

Some of you people reading this probably live in the suburbs in the good parts of town but I don't and I've always had a secret fear of fire because I live on the third floor and we don't have a fire escape and also when I was a kid, a family in our street got roasted to death from the wife burning fat in a frying pan and they couldn't get out, so when the door was locked I got scared some crazy person might be frigging about and when I get scared I get mad like when I get punched and I started to yell and hit the door because I had a lot of life in me and something special I still had to do before I died, namely fuck Candy Starr.

Loreen woke up with a jump.

"What the hell's going on?"

"OPEN THIS FUCKING DOOR OPEN IT SOMEONE OPEN THIS DOOR YOU HEAR ME OUT THERE OPEN THIS DOOR!" And I start hitting on the wall to the room next to me at the same time.

"For Christ's sake Joe what's the matter?"

"Someone's locked the frigging door, OPEN THIS FRIGGING DOOR OR I'LL SMASH IT DOWN YOU BASTARDS." And I was just going to really start kicking the door down when the landlord (you remember the property-owning comedian with the witty repartee) answers from outside and he's talking in a real nice pleasant tone of voice.

"Something the matter Andretti?"

"Open this door. Someone's locked this door from the outside."

"I locked door."

"WHAT!, WELL FRIGGING OPEN IT!"

"You stay home a little, we got things discuss with a friend of mine. He's coming in half hour. You wait a little."

"YOU OPEN THIS DOOR YOU COMMIE BASTARD OR I'LL SMASH IT DOWN AND YOU TOO." His grand-parents left Russia in the nineties to escape the pogroms he told me, so I called him a commie bastard.

"I take you court for damage to my property."

"You can't hold me like this, I have to go to work."

"You have afternoon shift Wednesday."

"Cunt."

"I be back don't worry. And don't try window, I got my dog out there." And he goes away.

"COME BACK HERE YOU CUNT YOU CAN'T DO THIS IT'S AGAINST THE LAW, I'LL GET YOU DEPORTED, THIS IS AMERICA . . . ." But the bastard wasn't there, and no-one else sounded like they were coming either.

Loreen says, "What's the matter with that shit anyway?"

"I owe the guy rent."

And I did. I'd been spending a lot on magazines lately to do a total redecoration of my room, and a couple of new movies with Candy had just come out and I'd seen them three or four times each and I'd given a whole lot to the club to help buy a new projector, so I was a bit short and owed a couple of weeks rent. Four actually.

"But he can't keep you locked up. And what about me, it's kidnapping, he can't do that."

"Dirty foreign commie cunt." My own parents had come over from Italy in 1949 but I was so mad I wasn't thinking along those type of reasonable lines at all.

"What are you going to do?"

"Phone the President."

"What about me Joe, I got to go."

"I'm not stopping you."

"Oh fuck off."

"Fuck you too."

I looked out of the window and the landlord's Doberman starts to bark. Would you believe it, I'm three floors up and this animal hears me and starts to bark. Years ago dogs used to hunt in the fields, now they protect dirty commie foreign landlord's property. Beautiful world. I started to think if I had any poison I could put it on some food and throw it out of the window and then lower myself down by tying the sheets and the blankets together without people on the lower floors seeing me and . . . .

So we both stayed in my room and were unhappy. Life is hard and then you die.

About twenty minutes later the key turns in the lock and the landlord comes in and I'm just going to crush him into a small pile of dirt when his friend comes in and has to bend his head to get through the door and turn his shoulders sideways to get his body in. So I immediately change my strategy and revert to a verbal assault.

"Who the fuck do you think you are, locking me in here? And this young lady." If he's been any kind of a gentleman that should have reduced him to a guilty, apologetic heap, the landlord I mean, but they both looked pretty confident.

"Hello Andretti I want you meet my nephew."

"Hi," I said, looking up.

The giant was looking at the pictures on the walls and couldn't have heard me. 'Deaf bastard,' I thought. And the landlord smiles at some funny idea in his stupid Russian head and this is where Loreen makes a tactical mistake because she walks up to him with her hand pulled back to slap his face and she's saying, "You cunt how dare you . . .", and the giant pushes her away with one hand and she hits the wall really hard and falls down next to it and starts to cry, and seeing my decision to revert to a strategy of verbal assault proved correct before my eyes, I decide to stick to it, which Loreen was pretty angry about later on.

"Hey wait a minute . . ."

"You owe my uncle four weeks rent," says the giant deaf bastard.

"Look just because . . . ."

"I told you 'bout it Andretti and I warned you and you just don't do nothing 'bout it," says the comedian and every time the giant deaf bastard speaks the uncle fills in the picture, like some fucking press agent for some foreign film star at Kennedy airport.

"O.K. I'll pay you, I told you I'd pay you for Christ's sake."

"How soon?" asks the jolly green giant.

"Look I don't kn . . . ."

"We don't want no empty promises no more Andretti we want how much, how often, how soon. Comprehensive."

"You fucking coward Joe Andretti!" Loreen was recovering and doing her bit to help things go smooth. "You fuck Candy Starr? Not this side of the revolution you won't, fink," says Loreen from her corner.

I made some quick calculations in my head, all the time watching the giant who was probably also kept under the table when he was a child.

"Say four weeks, no five weeks say five weeks, I can definitely pay you in five weeks." Bang goes five weeks of my private life to the debt collector and the jolly green giant, the brains of the outfit. Einstein turns his head to look at his uncle.

"O.K?"

"Honestly that's the best I can . . . ."

"That's completely satisfactory," says the witty one.

But the jolly green giant is a mind reader as well as a genius.

"Don't think of running some place. We'll find you."

Now there was one word in what he said that I didn't like and though the uncle was filling in again, I didn't hear him because I was concentrating on this word and the word was 'we'. Now I don't mind running away from 'I' because you're in front and you know where 'I' is, but when it's 'we' you might be running from one 'we' and you think he's far away and all the time you're running into the arms of the other 'we' or a number of 'wes'. They might find out from Loreen where I was headed or from the club and I saw myself all chewed up on Candy's door-step and as she opens the door I say, "I've come to fuck you" through the piece of lung which is hanging out of my mouth, and she screams and L.A. Law find the guilty parties and I thank them from my wheelchair, from which they smilingly tell me that I should be getting out of in twenty or thirty years. Because I had a deep certainty that this 'we' was more than just the giant and his uncle, because property is a very valuable asset.

"Hey, come on here, let's be cool about this thing, O.K."—(I have become Mr. Reasonable)—"What are you talking about, I ain't going anywhere, where would I go, for Christ's sake?" And I thought everything was settled. Wrong.

"You called my uncle a dirty commie bastard," says the giant.

And before the comedian can fill in, he punches me across the room confirming my thoughts about 'we'. Through my bleeding nose I hear him say, "we vote Republican." Then they both go out. Loreen didn't come over to help me.

When I was a kid I went through a bad time at home once with my father and I thought about it for a long time and finally made the big decision. I was going to leave home. Who needed it, who cared, fuck my parents anyway I thought, I was going out there, I was going to make it on my own. The police picked me up at the first subway. The cop says to me, "Hey young fella, where'd'you think you're going?" I say, "I'm leaving home, it's a free country ain't it?" I'm seven years old, right. He says to me, "You ain't going nowhere, kid." And here I was again, taking another most important decision and right at the start of my most important journey ever and again fate steps across me and closes the trap.

Life is hard and then you die.

Chapter Four

Well, it wasn't that bad though, what the hell. O.K. so originally I was going to fuck Candy that week and now I'd have to wait five weeks 'till I'd paid the comedian and King Kong their money and my nose healed before I see her. So what, I'd waited so long, five weeks wouldn't make the difference. So I worked all the over-time I could get, I cut out the movies and the magazines and girls (Loreen stayed sore and told me to piss off anyway) and I almost cut out food and I walked a lot instead of paying for transportation.

You know what a hospital porter does? He's like a station porter only instead of luggage he pushes stiffs or injured or dying or sick people. He pushes them to the operating theatre and back to the ward, to the ward and back to the operating theatre, to the morgue and not back, he pushes oxygen, laundry, food, towels, everything you need in a hospital. Except for the walls he pushes practically the whole hospital around to different other parts of the hospital and I just did a lot more pushing every day.

People were dying around me, people were getting better, people were having babies and losing them, people were having their hearts transplanted, the great dramas of human life were being played out all around me, for all I know they'd invented the cure for cancer, I was only thinking about one thing.

Candy.

Days passed I didn't know which days they were, each day was the same, work—sleep, work—sleep, work—sleep, work—sleep. But I did tell Mike about my plan.

I guess if I thought about it Mike was the best friend I had. Not that I'd known him longest because he hadn't been too long at the hospital, and I had people I went out with from the club and even from when I was a kid from the neighbourhood and from school and from all over. But they were more acquaintances, because acquaintances are about knowing and friends are about feeling and I had very good feelings for Mike.

Mike was a porter like me though he was a qualified engineer but he couldn't get no engineer's job, maybe because he was black, and we used to sit in the locker-room and smoke and talk and sometimes we'd go for a drink or movie or bowling. I think he liked me because I was reasonably anti-bull-shit.

"So you want to fuck Candy Starr." And then he thought about it. That's what I liked about the guy, he didn't just come right out and say the first stupid thing that came into his head, just telling me what he thought everyone else would think about it or what he thought I'd like to hear or anything corny, he thought about it.

"Well, they all said I'd never make an engineer."

"You ain't yet." I said. He laughed. He took a puff of his cigarette.

"I think it's O.K."

And that's all he said but I knew he understood my feelings about it. I didn't tell nobody else at the hospital about what I had in mind though one of the other porters when he saw me doing so many extra shifts said, "Saving up to visit that Candy Starr?" and I got a real sweat for a minute but then I saw from his face that it was a guess because most people there knew about my love for Miss Starr and they used to rib me about it, especially the nurses, some of who I'd been out with on dates and even for longer. Nurses don't usually go out with porters, they prefer the sharp instrument of a senior surgeon or the antiseptic needles of the consultant, but maybe I'd got a reputation because of my interest in Candy and anyway I was pretty confident about women in the bed department. Whatever it was, I had studied the anatomy of quite a few of the nurses at first hand and we always stayed friendly after.

I read in a paper somewhere that they did a survey which showed that nurses were the most feminine of all groups of women which I don't know if it's true but I do know that they're the most beautiful group of people that I ever met. They're very sensitive and kind and most of all they're very optimistic about life and enjoy it and are very positive.

One day just after I'd told Mike about Candy and me, I was pushing an old man down the corridor to his ward when an old flame passes me—beautiful red hair, beautiful memories. She smiles at me.

"You're spending a lot of time with us these days Joe."

"Can't keep away from you, honey."

She went away laughing. Corny huh?

So I was working my arse off.

Finally just like I thought after around five weeks I'd saved up the extra cash to pay the double act what I owed them. I knocked on the door of the wittier one.

"Come in."

I went in. King Kong was paying a visit.

"I got the cash."

King Kong counts, the wittier one watches like a starving peasant watching Henry the Eighth feeding his face. (Charles Laughton. The girl who worked on Off-Broadway took me to see the movie, very good.) King Kong nods, the witty one flashes me a sick grin full of black, broken ivory.

"I hear you going to visit Missus Candy Starr the movie person, very funny, very amusing."

I had a cab waiting for me downstairs with my case all packed. I didn't pack much, I thought I'd wait and see what the fashion was out there on the other coast. I looked at the witty one and smiled a grin back at the ass-hole.

"Rumour, a rumour, a joke between some friends of mine," and I head for the door. When I get there I make sure my body is already outside and I stick my head back round the door and I shout at the pair of 'em.

"You fuckin' pair of Republican, grasping ass-holes, I hope your mothers die of cancer in agony in your arms," and I fly down the stairs four at a time, into the cab and away before King Kong can get his fuckin fat head under the door jam.

So I'm on the road to the airport and the cab stops at a red light and I see Candy.

So I'm on the road to the airport and the cab stops at a red light and I see Candy. (Yeah, just in case you missed it the first time). My mind went into a complete confusion. Before when I'd had dreams about just meeting her in the street. I saw myself walk up to her and say 'hello, how are you, Miss Starr' or running like a lunatic to catch her or whatever, but it was always an action scene, but that's not how it was now. I jumped out of the cab but then I just stood there thinking one million seven hundred thousand things in three seconds. 'That's Candy Starr why hasn't she got a coat on it's too cold she isn't in Hollywood she's here has she heard about me what's she doing walking around like a normal person her hair is blowing in the breeze she's shopping don't they have what she wants in Hollywood what if she gets mugged by someone who doesn't recognise her where are the crowds why shouldn't she just be visiting a relative why isn't she working is her career on the slide where are the photographers has she been doing a modelling job in the park I'm fifty yards away from her ass,' and then a big black sedan pulled up next to her and she got in and it drove away.

I just stood there. I was shaking. I shook. I just stood there looking after the car. I shook. The cabbie starts yelling, at first I didn't hear him, then I just paid him what he wanted, I can't even remember how much, he drives away cursing, I'm just standing there shaking.

After a few minutes my thoughts started to slow down, but I still didn't move. I thought, 'I've blown it. I plan the biggest thing in my whole life, the most important thing that ever happened to me, the thing that I want more than anything else, I even get over the barrier that life has put in front of me in the shape of King Kong and his handler, then it's handed to me on a plate, the woman practically falls into my arms and I blow it.' (An old lady with glasses and a stick and grey hair stopped in front of me and asked me if everything was alright but I didn't say anything, I went on looking where the car had pulled up and she walked on). I thought some more. 'She was right there near me, next to me, if I'd just run if I'd just shouted . . . . Shit, well anyway I can still do what I was going to do before, you can't find a black saloon in the whole of New York, I'll just have to fly out to L.A. like I was going to anyway and hope she's back from New York.'

And then I remembered the licence number of the car. I had the scene in my head like a photograph, Candy, the car, the trees, the cab, the people, and I just moved my eyes in my mind a little to the left of Candy's legs and read off the number.

I went a little crazy.

I jumped up and down yelling 'yippee' and waving my arms all over the place and a few people looked at me. I was happy, I'd made it, it was going to be alright, success, relief, fulfillment. All I had to do was trace the owner of the car, go to the house and knock on the door and to get to the door all I had to do was go to the place that has the records of all car numbers, which is the police . . . .

I don't know how you feel about it, but the way I grew up you didn't go to the cops for help about anything, not even if there was money in it. Not even to trace your long lost cousin who has your million dollars. Not even to find Candy Starr. To us, cops were enemy. To us cops meant interference, suspicion, a kicking in the cellar under the watchful eye of our friendly local sergeant. "Not so it shows, stupid." He didn't want our girlfriends to be upset about how beat up we looked on our next date. "Just hate to spoil your fun, kid." Bang' in the gut, bang! in the kidney. To us the cops meant being picked up on the

street at night because Mr Livorno had chased his wife
with a kitchen knife which he did regularly once a month
and the police were investigating, which meant they were
snooping around. They pull up next to you, two of 'em get
out, one's got a gun, the other frisks you, then into the
car.

"Hi, Joey."

You don't answer. (Next day at school with the big
men; "I didn't tell 'em a thing. They roughed me up a
little, but I just kept my mouth shut, which is my right.")

"Hey Joey, I'm talking to you. He's gone a little deaf
Tom, wax in his ears, clear his ear out will you."

Bang! on the side of your head. Your ear sings
inside. You feel the blood on your neck. (No worries
about marking you outside now, you were obstructing
an officer in the pursuit, etc. "The witness is lying, your
honour, as officer Smith will also testify. We attempted
to question the witness while in the pursuance of our
enquiries regarding the crime, and the witness refused
to co-operate and then voluntarily smashed his head
several times against the wing-mirror of the police vehicle
and finally broke his own arm by hitting it several times
across the top of a fire-hydrant."

"This is a very unusual affair, Sergeant Green."

"I'm afraid this is the kind of individual we're dealing
with here, your honour.")

"Can you hear me now, Joey?"

You mutter to show it's under duress. "Yeah."

"Yeah, that's right. What do you know about this
Livorno character?"

"I don't know him." Bang! You can move your loose
front tooth with your tongue a little.

"Don't spit that blood over my uniform, kid," says Sergeant Green. (Poor Mrs Green, her washing machine's not fixed yet, she's working her fingers to the bone and naturally her husband is concerned for her.) "Now listen you bum, what do you mean you don't know Livorno, he lives next to you."

"We don't talk with them."

"Why not? You're all wops together ain't you?"

"Don't call me a fucking wop!"

Bang!

"Why don't you talk to them kid?"

"My mother says Mrs Livorno is no good."

"Sure your mother's not covering up because old man Livorno is giving her one."

"Don't talk about my ma like that you fucking . . ."

Bang!

They didn't give a fuck about Livorno and his wife. They were just getting to know what went on in the area. Intelligence-gathering.

But I had to trace the number of the black saloon and the only way I knew to trace a car was through the police and as you can see, I didn't trust 'em. I could see a whole big deal developing with them wanting to know why I wanted the number and then maybe there was something dubious going on in the background of these car people, and the next thing you know the boys in blue have me down at the station as a suspect and hassle-hassle, and so on. You know, the innocent member of the public doing his citizen's duty goes to give evidence in a case of murder, next thing you know he's the top suspect, the police don't have anything else to go on, they build a case against him, a finger-print is deposited here, some DNA there, a cartridge-case elsewhere, and the guy gets caged for a million years because he opened his big mouth. Don't laugh, it happens.

So I needed a cop I was friendly with, which I didn't have, or someone I was friendly with who was friendly with a cop. And that—Jesus, Mary and Joseph, it came into my head the second I thought about it, there is a God, there is justice, there is love in the universe—THAT I HAD!!! Chris. You remember, the body-carpenter, star of stage, screen and hack-saw. He had contacts in the force, he could do something devious for an old friend, he, mad, crazy, kicked-under-the-table Chris could save my fucking life! Only thing, I hadn't seen him for a couple of years since I stopped seeing Julie, the girl who made the costumes and took me to see Henry the Eighth.

Now I hear a few of you thinking, 'That's funny, how come the hack-saw-man-turned-actor is friendly with the police, wasn't he some sort of a criminal before?' But that only shows you live in the world of the green lawns and green trees and green-backs, because what you think is a lot of horse-shit because that is not how it works one little bit. People think and the TV people pretend to think that the world of the law-breaker and the world of the law-enforcer are quite separate. Wrong. Not that I don't know that the police put criminals behind bars, but the whole thing is much more mixed up than that, where the information the police get leads them to the top criminals, who it's easier to make a deal with than arrest, so the detective goes on the payroll and it's now in his interests to make sure, for instance, that drugs get sold not stopped, and he's mixing with the top people now, which is where you get the connection between Chris and his model friend and show business, and politicians come to the parties, and the whole thing of right and wrong becomes what I see in the papers the other day during the investigations the CIA call a grey area. And if you want to know, Chris told me he paid off a detective 2000 dollars in connection with another little disagreement he had with some guy in the line of business, which spoiled this guy's chances of becoming a husband and father except by way of adoption, and that is the way it goes in those circles, as some of you know who are reading this right now (though most of you don't and most of you don't want to know anyway, because you <u>do</u> know deep inside and it makes you sleep uneasy in your satin-covered bed next to your satin-covered wife.)

I didn't have an address or phone-number for Chris because I only met him socially, nor for his girl, so I went straight down to the little theatre where Julie used to work.

It was a converted grocery store and when I got inside, there were the same jeans and black sweaters and long haired men and black curtains but I didn't recognise any of the faces. I sort of liked the place even though they came on very strong with all that Meaning-of-Life type of atmosphere and when you're just a working guy you know the meaning of life, which is making enough money to feed your face and I wasn't surprised that most of them didn't because half of them were living on their lawyer, doctor, executive fathers' hand-outs. Still, I guess in their own way they were against all of that 'there's no business like show business, everything is beautiful, laugh and the world laughs with you, happy unhappy families' Broadway bull-shit as Julie explained to me, and I agreed with her about that. I saw a play there once written by the Minister of Culture of the Black Panthers when they were still going fifty years ago about black consciousness she told me. It was sort of a 'I want to fuck Diana Ross' play. I liked it. Anyway a girl with brown lip-stick told me that Julie was working for a big Broadway costume-maker now, and she gave me the address.

So much for the meaning of life thing.

When I got to this top costume place it was the kind of place you'd expect Mae West to come out from behind one of the pillars and silk curtains and ask someone to peal her a grape. Julie was working in one of the rooms on the sixth floor at the back sewing some red shiny material on a machine.

"Hello Julie," I said.

She looked at me and behind her eyes I could see Cadillacs and board meetings and French perfume and barbecue parties with white musicians in white suits playing rock-and-roll with the rock and the roll taken out of it and gambling tables with tits hanging over them out of million dollar dresses called creations. She looked at my suit as though it smelled of something bad.

"Oh. Hello Joe. What can I do for you, hun?"

What could she do for me, hun? When she was looking for the meaning of life she knew what she could do for me and she knew what I could do for her too, believe me.

"I'm trying to find Chris, but I don't have any way to get him, can you give me his number, or Hazel's (her friend the model).

"Oh, I see. Well I don't have Chris's number and Hazel's is ex-directory, I don't know if she'd want me to . . . ."

This was the girl who told me to read 'The Greening of America' because it would change my life. Oh boy, daddy is proud of her now.

She gave me Hazel's address eventually, because after all I had known Hazel and she supposed it would be alright. When I left, she smiled down on me from a great height.

If you saw Hazel, you'd recognise her from the super-model fashion magazines. When I knew her she was very big. She fucked English Dukes, French Counts, Greek ship owners, American rock singers and Chris for his big prick. She spoke to me through the door when I rang the bell. After all, I might rape her.

"Who is it?"

"It's Joe Andretti."

"Who's that? I don't know you."

"I used to take Julie out with you and Chris." She still didn't open the door.

"What do you want?"

"I have to see Chris." Now she opened the door wide. All kinds of people wanted to see Chris and some of them wanted to kill him because he cut their friends' arms off with a hack-saw, and she would have phoned him if there was any trouble waiting for him.

"Why do you want to see him?"

Hazel was a tall as me and what I'd call skinny, but even without make-up and with her hair in a mess, she was a beautiful woman. She had a night-robe on which she hadn't fastened and I could see the inside of her thighs, her box, her belly and the inside of her tiny tits. I read in the papers once where she's stripped in a restaurant. Chris puts his prick on the table, she puts her body. Maybe her father kept her under the table also.

54

"I want him to help me trace a car." I couldn't take my eyes off her box.

"Are you after a fuck? Is this just an excuse?"

I was in too much of a hurry to find Candy and also I didn't think I could push a trolley at the hospital with one good arm and one stump after Chris had finished with me, if he ever found out. I didn't see Candy being attracted by the stump either.

She gave me an address in the village where Chris had moved to be amongst the artists. When I went away from her place, I felt a feeling of disgust. She hated herself so much. If you told her you loved her, I think she would have laughed and taken your prick out and sucked it. If anyone could, she'd have changed gold back into lead.

You think I was pissed off criss-crossing New York from one place to the next? I was flying, I was firm, I was crisp. Three steps to go to see Candy, two steps to go, one . . . .

Chris was very low when I found him. He used to get like that. In one day he could change half a dozen times, one minute swinging his prick, the next sitting on a bench not speaking, biting the skin round his nails, then the next minute carrying Hazel on his shoulders with her belly in his face, then say he was going some place and leave me with the two girls. I must say, Hazel used to be very good about it. She knew where to find him late at night and what to do, I mean get him out of his blues. Or if she couldn't she'd go and fuck a Duke. Chris asked me in, he didn't ask what I wanted or how I'd been or why he hadn't heard from me, he just told me to get myself a drink and then he sat down in an arm-chair and stared at his shoes. I asked him how he was, he grunted O.K. I asked him if he's been doing any acting, he said he's just finished something, he didn't say what. His big, square body just filled the chair and his baby face looked at his shoes in despair. I told him I needed help tracing a car, could he find out for me through his connections. He mumbled he'd see what he could do. But he wasn't really listening.

I started to get worried because if he stayed like this I'd never get through to him, and my lead might get cold, might leave town, might vanish. It's not that I was scared or anything, because when he was like this he never went berserk, only when he felt good, but you couldn't shift him out of his mood. You couldn't tell him to snap out of it, things weren't so bad, let's forget it and go out and have a good time. It just happened or didn't happen, so in desperation I told him what it was all about, and it worked. It was like someone turning on the current. Somehow the idea tickled him.

"You want to what?"

I repeated my plans for Candy and me.

"You're fucking crazy, man. Man, you're crazy."

He was really starting to sound like what he thought an actor sounded like, he never said 'man' when I knew him. The hack-saw man. Such a strong personality. Such a weak personality really.

"You're fucking insane, man. You should have been inside the funny farm with me. You tell that to one of them trick cyclists, they'll fill you full of largactyl, modicate, everything." And he was laughing fit to bust. He had a beautiful laugh, out of control, the whole of him laughing.

"You can't do that," he managed to say. "How can you do that"

"Well, you ball Hazel."

"Yeah. But Candy Starr, I mean. Who's next, the president's mother?"

And he was laughing himself all around the room.

"Hey, do you think Candy'd like some of this?" And out of his trousers comes Hazel's pleasure, the boa-constrictor. "Think she's a vegetarian, like some cucumber?"

"If you trace the number for me, I'll ask her."

"Andretti, you're a freak, you can't do it."

I felt like saying some people can't cut someone's arm off with a hack-saw.

"How are you going to do it, man, for Christ's sake?"

"Same as always. Find her, ask her and then do it."

"What if she says no?"

"I'll keep trying."

"What if she still won't?"

"I don't know. She will."

He stood there, shaking his head at me in admiration, his prick forgotten for once, swaying slightly as he moved his head.

"Andretti, you're an original. If I'd 'a known I'd 'uve taken you with me to one or two heists I can think of. Listen, I might have something good coming up. Speed. Just driving. You interested?"

'EX-GANGSTER ACTOR ON DRUGS CHARGE. ASSOCIATE ASKS CANDY STARR TO STAND BAIL.'

"When I've fucked Candy I'll give it some consideration."

He promised to get me the information by mid-day the next day. I should phone him.

Walking down the stairs, he shouts after me, "When you work your way up to screwing the President's mother I want an invitation," and his laughter followed me into the street.

Chapter Five

I slept very badly that night, maybe 'cos I had a dream.
My father was building a house for the family on
a piece of waste ground. He'd got as far as putting
up the wooden beams and supports, but between the
frame-work he was building the walls out of stone, very
strong, like cottages he'd shown me in post-cards showing
the villages back home in Italy. He seemed to be very good
at the work, although my father was a leather worker in
real life, and he was enjoying himself and singing, but the
song he was singing was a religious song from the mass.
Where the front door was going to be, there was a hole in
the ground, long, like a grave, and I was lying in it, and
my mother was kneeling next to me singing a lullaby like
I was in a cradle, but at the same time she was pouring
cement on me, starting at my feet, and smoothing it over,
sort of levelling it off to the level of the earth. I was really
scared and trying to get out, but the cement round my
feet was hard and all I could do was sit up. My mother was
telling me to be a good boy and word hard like my father
and not to go out no more with any rough kids from the

neighbourhood and to go out and get a good job, and stuff like that. And all the time the cement was creeping up my body, till I was covered up even over my head, but I could still see out. Then my mother stood in the frame of wood where the door was gonna be and opened her might gown and showed me her body naked which was like Candy's, and she was smiling a grin, like an advertisement, and I could hear my sister's voice offering prizes if you won the competition, and the big prize was a million dollars and everlasting life. But my sister kept throwing wet sand in my eyes, so I couldn't see the TV screen too well through this curtain of sand, and I woke up rubbing my eyes and feeling upset and without energy.

I went out and got some breakfast and waited for the time to call Chris. I wasn't going in to work of course. I had better things to do.

I phoned Chris at twelve and he had traced the car to a house in Scarsdale. He was still laughing about it all when I put the phone down and headed for the station.

I was still a little upset about the dream when I got on the train but it started to wear off as my mind thought about other things. First, the name of the man who owned the car was Jimenez, and I went over in my head who he could be. Was he an agent, a personal manager, a friend, a producer, what? But I hadn't heard of a lot of Mexican or South American guys in that line of work. Maybe he was a doctor, and Candy went to see him and wouldn't be there no more, but then I decided against that, because no doctor picks you up in his car. I went over and over it, not because I saw the guy as a block to my hopes, but just because I didn't know, and I was anxious to know about what the set up would be out there.

Then I started to think about what Chris had said. Until he started asking me, I never thought seriously about Candy saying no to me, really, but he had set me thinking about it now, and I looked at the possibilities. Frankly I still didn't think she'd say no, but if she did, well I'd just ask her again and if she still said no, I'd leave it a couple of days and try again, and then if it was still no, I'd just have to think again and find some way round it, but for some reason I didn't treat her rejecting me as a serious possibility at all, I just felt it would work out O.K.

The house was up a long avenue with trees and the cars I could see were all Rolls Royce and Ferraris and that type and looked very comfortable. The house itself was almost hidden from the road by trees and it was set well back and had a long drive up to it. I just walked up to the door and rang the bell.

A man opened the door in a dark suit and short cut black hair dyed blonde like he was just back from the army and then joined a rock band or something. He didn't say anything.

"Mr Jimenez?" I asked.

"No, what do you want?"

"Well truthfully I came to see Miss Starr."

"There's no Miss Starr here. You've got the wrong place."

And he shut the door.

Now I hadn't honestly reckoned with Candy not being there, though I knew she might be just visiting, but it was the way he said it in his South American accent, he didn't say "She's not here anymore," or "She's just gone out," he said it like she'd never been there, and I didn't believe that, so either he was lying or Jimenez had dropped her off somewhere, and only he would know where, so I rang again. Back comes the South American marine pop singer.

"I told you you got the wrong house, buddy."

"Look, I have to speak to Mr Jimenez." I knew he was there because the New York Police Department said so, and there was the black saloon in the drive with the number plate I'd remembered near the park and gave to Chris.

"Who are you?"

A second guy now came to the door and looked over the shoulder of the first. He obviously wasn't in the combo, 'cos his hair was still black and quite long and combed back and thick and quite greasy.

"My name's Joe Andretti."

My guy looks back at the new one and then looks back at me.

"Wait here a minute." And he goes inside the house.

The new one stood and looked at he. He wasn't impolite exactly, but he wasn't respectful either. He sort of looked at me like I was a Coke bottle moving along the conveyor belt at the bottling plant in Rio. He could drink me and then throw me away, or just throw me away. I thought I'd do a little NYPD Blues on him.

"Has Miss Starr been gone long?"

The guy didn't answer. I began to feel that he'd dropped the option of drinking me. Now it was just throwing me away.

The blonde came back.

"Come in, Mr Andretti," I was on my way again.

They showed me into a room with dark wooden panels on the walls and a desk in it. The blonde pointed me to a chair and went out. The bottle-tester stayed with me, standing next to the door. One thing was for sure, this was no family home. Maybe a producer's or a backer. We'd see.

The blonde guy comes back after a few minutes with another man, who is about thirty-five and lean and small and he's wearing just a white shirt and slacks. The blonde guy stands next to the door on the other side, and the new, lean one walks past me to the desk and sits down also without saying hello. He puts his elbows on the desk and picks his fingers.

"Yes?" Also from south of the Rio Grande.

One thing this place wasn't was a bureau of information. When I asked the questions they told me nothing, and when they asked the questions they told me nothing. I thought about the positive thinking book and sat up a little straighter.

"Are you Mr Jimenez?"

"What do you want?" More positive, Andretti.

"I told your man here, I came to see Miss Starr, but . . . ."

"And you were told there is no such person at this address."

"Then I want to talk to Mr Jimenez. Look, are you Jimenez or not?" The guy wasn't looking too happy, I thought, and I was beginning to pick up.

I thought.

He says, "Who told you that a Mr Jimenez lived here?"

Why should I lie to the guy, if I told him I had proof of Jimenez living here, he might stop stalling. And Candy would be impressed with how I followed up my only lead.

I thought.

"The police traced him from the number on his car."

The lean one behind the desk stopped picking his fingers for a second. It was only for a second, but I seen it.

"Are you from the police?"

"Hell no, I . . . ."

"Then how did you procure their services? Are you a private investigator?"

"Of course I'm not a private in . . . ."

"The New York police do not customarily offer the service you have just described to the average citizen."

"I got it through a friend."

"What is his name?"

"Chris."

"Chris who?"

"Chris Angel."

"Ahhh." Things were looking up again, if the guy knew Chris, he probably was a producer, maybe Chris had acted in one of his movies. He was still talking quietly, re-picking his fingers, I thought we were making progress.

"So. Mr Angel gave you this address."

"That's right."

"And why did he send you here?" It was slipping away again.

"He didn't send me here, he only . . . ."

"You said he gave you this address."

"That's right."

"To see a Mr Jimenez."

"No!"

"I distinctly hear you say you wanted to see Mr Jimenez."

"I told you and your friends that I wanted to see Miss Starr, but you all said she wasn't here, so then I wanted to ask Mr Jimenez how to meet her. That's all I want, that's why I'm here, to get to see Miss Starr, now will someone just tell me where Mr Jimenez is, please, so we can stop the Spanish Inquisition and I can stop bothering you all, O.K." I was getting pissed.

The lean man thought for a moment, then looked up at the two men behind me who grabbed me, pulled me to my feet and started to search me and take what they found out of my pockets and put it in the desk. When I struggled, one of them twisted my arm behind my back and put his other arm around my throat and the other one went on with the search. I couldn't do much or say much, so I just kicked a little. I thought, who was this Jimenez, some fucking South American Howard Hughes or something, and why was he so suspicious?

When they finished, they stuffed me back into the chair and held me there by my shoulders when I tried to get up, though I wasn't struggling too hard 'cos I didn't want to make too much of a drama 'cos I wanted to get to Candy.

"Nothing," said the phoney blonde. I looked at the desk, my comb, my keys, some money, a pack of cigarettes, matches.

"You may take your things, Mr Andretti."

"Look, who do you think you are grabbing me and . . . ."

The lean one puts his fingers up to his lips and said "sssss".

"Wait one moment please," he says and walks out.

I'd had a belly full and I was now feeling very uneasy. I was beginning to get the same feeling I used to have when they got me in the police car when I was a kid. But I stayed because Candy was with Jimenez and Jimenez was here in this house, or at least he lived here and his car was here. So I didn't let my mind hear what my mind was telling me. I looked at the two body-guards meaning to show them with my face that I wouldn't forget theirs, but they didn't look scared. Then the lean man comes back and now he's smiling.

"Mr Jimenez will see you." Well thank Christ for that, progress.

The two heavies walked me through the house and out the back into the garden. It was a beautiful big garden with fruit trees and roses and a big lawn big enough for a dance floor. I smelt the flowers and I smelt the sun and I was better. They walked me over to a fat man who was putting some string around a young tree and fixing it to a pole. He was about thirty-five too, dressed in his shirt sleeves and the thing about him was his hair, which was white and very thick, though he has a long moustache which is still black. He turns round to look at me with a big smile on his face, really genuine, pleased to see me, like he was a long lost cousin, his face was very brown, hook nose, fat jaw-line, black moustache, white hair.

And I knew these guys ran drugs. Don't ask me how I knew, but that moment looking at the fat one fixing up the rose-tree and the whole set up so far and the dark skin and the black moustache, I knew.

"Hello Mr Andretti, how are you, so you come to see me."

"I just want to know if you can tell me when Miss Starr is, that's all, that's the only reason I came. That's the truth, Mr. Jimenez."

"How is Chris there days? They tell me he's an actor, big film star or something, how is he?"

"He's OK, Mr Jimenez, but he doesn't know you I know, because he never said nothing about knowing you at all."

"Some people know me, some people don't know me. Little people don't know me. That's how I like it." Smiling, reasonable, a man in his early to middle years tending his roses in the sun in his own back yard with his black moustache and dark skin. So what's wrong with that? Answer, drug-running.

He turns and calls to the other side of the garden.

"Honey, come a minute."

And out of the roses comes Candy. And I must have jumped because the dark heavy pulls a gun and aims it straight-arm at my head.

But he didn't shoot.

And it wasn't Candy

When I was about twelve years old, my parents took me to see a show around Christmas. We sat in the back of the theatre in the cheaper seats. One of the acts was a man and a girl dancing and the girl was about sixteen years old, and I fell in love with her completely from the first second I saw her. She was small and slim with one of those dance costumes up to her fanny, her hair was combed back off her face into a long tail at the back, her cheeks were red like the country sun at night and her body was a white young tree, whipping and flashing and flying through the air, and standing bent over backwards on the arm of the male dancer. I loved her, I was flooded with love and aching for her, and full of guilt about my dirty feelings, as I sat between my mother and father. I looked at the rest of the show, but I didn't see it, all I saw was my girl in my mind and all I felt were my feelings of love and longing. We went home after the show, I was in a daze. My mother asked me if I liked the show, I just said yes, and went up to my room and battered my little prick to pieces for the love of this girl. To me she was an angel on earth, she was pure, she was sweet, she was everything good and gentle and beautiful that god had ever created, in who at that time I still believed. And I had to see her again, (and for ever, I thought at the time). Of course I had no ideas of going to see her back-stage, I didn't know nothing about that, I just wanted to see the show again, but I couldn't tell my mother that. How could I tell my mother, she'd have been disgusted and told me to tell the priest at confession, so I stole some money from her purse, which I had never done before, and I told her I was going to see a friend, and I went back to the theatre.

I bought an expensive seat this time and I sat in the third row and I waited. The show was the same as before, of course, but again I didn't really see it, I was waiting for goodness, purity and light. And when she finally came on, she was a forty year old (she looked ninety to me) ex-ballet dancer with scrawny legs and a pointed nose. The youthful, summer glow was rouge, the lithe figure a hard-edged, taut, boney rope of over-trained muscle, the innocent eyes outlined in mascara, and I could see the bones of her top ribs over her empty breasts.

I was shattered. I couldn't believe it. At first I thought it was another girl, but the name on the programme was the same. Annabelle. I didn't stay for the rest of the show. I went home. I tried to masturbate again to the image of my original fantasy, but the reality of that earth-bound, breathless professional up there had crushed the dream for ever.

I had made a terrible mistake. What I could not see from a distance, I had invented.

And now, twenty-five years later, I done it again.

If I said the girl who came through the roses looked like Candy it would be true and not true. Overall she did look like her, but in every detail she didn't. Where Candy's breasts were in proportion to her body, this woman was top heavy. Where Candy's hips swelled to a beautiful roundness, she was too narrow. Where Candy's chin stood firm again after the dip down from her incredible cheeks, this one was pinched. Everything, everything miss the mark. But from fifty yards . . . .

All I wanted to do was leave. 'Excuse me, terribly sorry, begging your pardon, sorry to have troubled you, nothing to worry about, a case of mistaken identity, an error of vision, yes I will get some glasses and a white stick, yes I will be more careful in future, good-bye, farewell, toddle-oo, aufwiedersehn.' All I had to do was to convince four drug hoodlums, a gun and a whore that I meant them no harm. And that pigs can fly . . . .

"Is this the lady you wanted to meet?" the moustache was saying.

Some question. Mike Tyson asks you if the rumour is true that you want to ball his wife.

"Look Mr Jimenez, sir, I saw this lady near Central Park and I thought she was Candy Starr, who I'm trying to contact, and be honest, you can see she looks a lot like her and I just followed her here, but I see now that she isn't the other one and that you were all telling the truth when you told me that Miss Starr didn't live here, and it's just been a mistake, and I'm truly sorry for the inconvenience I've caused you all, and of course any embarrassment to the lady, and most of all any inconvenience, and of course any embarrassment." And could see that he didn't believe a fucking word of it.

He turned to the whore.

"Do you know this gentleman, honey?"

She shook her pretty head. I started to explain again, hopelessly.

"No, look, you don't understand, of course she doesn't know me, because of course . . . ."

Jimenez turned to finish tying his tree.

"Find out who is this bum," he growled, and something very hard hit me on the back of the head, and I woke up in a small room, which I thought first was a work-room, but which I soon realised wasn't because though it had a work bench and a chair, there was no tools or nails or materials, but a vice was on the work-bench. And there were dark stains on the vice. The door was locked.

Are you thinking what I thought after I woke up? That rights. It's 2014. <u>IT'S 2014 FOR CHRIST'S SAKE, THINGS LIKE THIS DON'T HAPPEN TODAY!</u> I mean for god's sake, it's 2014, 2014 A.D—After Dachau. 2014, A.C.—After Capone. 2014, A.K.—After Kennedy. 2014, A.T.D.O.H.R.—After The Declaration of Human Rights. I mean, I said to the light bulb hanging above me, it's the time of women's liberation, of black liberation, of gay liberation, of Puerto Rican liberation, everyone's getting liberated, everywhere oppression is being beaten back. Nixon showed his ass, the C.I.A. showed it's ass, this is not the dark ages, truth is bursting through the curtain, this is not the depression, this is not prohibition, of course we know that shady goings-on go on, but N.Y.P.D. Blues and L.A. Law and the rest are on the case and they're winning, and if they <u>are</u> going on, some of these bad things, we don't meet it, I mean you and me, ordinary folk, honest folk, we don't meet it, and if someone at a party points out someone and says 'he's big in the rackets', you turn round and you see a respectable man in a light grey suit, you don't see pistols and blood and dead bodies on the Persian carpet. I know, I know, of course you have muggings and drive-by shootings and young kids dying of drug overdoses, and prostitution and a lot of things need looking at, but <u>JESUS CHRIST, ITS 2014, AND THEY DON'T HAPPEN TO ME!!!!!!</u>

But they do and they did. I'm not crazy, I'm not a high-jacker, I'm not a hoodlum, I'm not a terrorist, I'm not anything more than you are, you, fella, yes, you now coming in on the train from Scarsdale this morning and reading this on the way to the office, but this is what happened to me on your patch.

H   E   L   P

I knew what they were thinking, and I knew what was going to happen now, (forgive me father for I have sinned.) They didn't believe my story and they thought I had some connection with a criminal organisation, (oh merciful God, maker of heaven and earth, look down on thy humble servant Joe Andretti), and they were going to find out what I was really after, and then they would waste me, or send me home without some important part of my body like my heart, (take pity on him in his hour of need, for in the valley of the shadow of death, only thou canst lighten our darkness). And the trouble was that whatever part of me they squeezed to a pulp in the vice, (oh blessed virgin, mother of our Lord Jesus Christ), even if I told them the truth a thousand times if I lived that long, (you who have seen the suffering of your own son on the cross for the sake of all men), they thought they knew that I was lying, and so they'd go on squeezing, (take pity on this other son, Joe Andretti). And even if I invented a story to stop the pain, (dear Saint Francis, I know we haven't talked for a bit), then they'd either kill me straight away, (but I have fallen into the rapids of the river of life), or torture me some more to find out the rest, (bring me back to the straight way of the lord of happiness. And please try to get a few more of the Saints and anybody else together and GET ME OUT OF THIS).

After about ten minutes they came, the phoney blonde, the greasy black-haired one and the lean one with the grin. One of them had a pail of water which he threw over me in case I was still a bit dazed from the bang on the head, (they wanted me to experience the full effect of the pain, of course) and then the lean one starts the interrogation.

"What's your name?"

"What? I told you . . . ."

"What's your name?"

"I told you my name. Look . . ."

"Who sent you?"

"Nobody sent me, I came to see if . . . ."

"Is Angel working for Portillo's people now?"

"What? Who's Portillo, listen, honest, I don't know no Portillo, I was just . . . . ?"

The guy took a stone out of his pocket and held it for me to take.

"Feel that."

I took the stone. Now I was really worried. He was crazy as well as insane.

He took the stone back from me and put it in the vice and turned the handle while he held the stone there with his other hand. After a few turns the stone broke into pieces.

"We're going to start with putting your fingers in. Now what's you name?"

Basically I had two problems. One was technical and one was mental. The technical problem was that there isn't a machine which shows if someone are definitely telling the truth (lie detectors ain't really proof). If there was such a machine, and these guys had one, they could have wired up my head and looked at the little screen or whatever, and seen that I was a man of my word. And the mental problem was that these FUCKING PEOPLE WERE SO FUCKING STUPID, THEY COULDN'T EVEN WORK OUT THAT IF I KNEW THEM AND CAME TO DO THEM HARM, I WOULDN'T COME ALONE AND UNARMED, YOU FUCKING STUPID FUCKING INSANE CREEPS!!! I decided not to waste my precious unsqueezed moments worrying that the progress of civilisation had been a little slower than I had hoped in the development of truth-detecting machines just at that moment and decided to try reasoning.

"Look, do you guys really think that if I was after Mr Jimenez or whatever, that I would just arrive at the front door alone without a gun and start telling you all some stupid story . . . ."

The two heavies threw me into the chair and tied me to it with straps so I couldn't move, then they moved the chair near the vice and one of them sat on me while the other grabbed my arm and held it over the vice and the lean man also took the hand and they stuck my first finger in the vice and closed it on the finger.

A short time after all of this, I was sitting in the subway, and a woman next to me was talking to her friend and saying that men didn't know what it was to suffer because it was women who actually had the child, and that no man could understand because they didn't know what pain was, and I started crying and spat in this woman's eye. It was really a horrible thing to do, which I would never have done before, but the way she was yapping on about pain and men not understanding just made me flip. And for a long time after, if people talked about pain, I used to cry, and I used to worry that a part of my head had a screw loose, because they say that more bombs were dropped on Hanoi in a few days than in the whole of the second world war, but all the bombs that were ever dropped in the whole world in the whole of time were nothing to what that vice did to me. I can't describe it to you, because it's like trying to describe God to someone who doesn't know what you're talking about, but I can tell you that it was the most awful thing that I could ever imagine could happen to a human being.

What they did was first they squeezed my finger for a quite short time, and then they'd stop and ask me a question, and I was crying and screaming and I couldn't even talk or understand what they said. So then they would start again, and stop, and again and stop. I don't know exactly what I said, but I guess I was screaming that I didn't know anything, and begging them to stop and stuff like that. Then my head cleared for a second and I screamed that I'd tell them, I'd tell them. Anything to stop the pain. Anything to stop that eternity of pain even for a second.

"I . . . er . . . I was sent . . . er . . . you were right . . . er . . . I was sent to kill Jimenez," and I was weeping all the while I talked, "Portillo . . . er . . . Portillo wanted him killed, so . . . er . . . so he got Chris to find someone to . . .

er . . . do the job, and . . . er . . . he got me and told me that . . . er . . . that . . . er . . . the Mafia wanted Jimenez out of the way and . . . er . . . I was the man because I . . . because I am a karate expert and . . . er . . . I don't need a gun which . . . which could look suspicious. And that's the truth, please believe me, please, oh God, please, please." And the horrible thing about it was, that I didn't know enough about the truth of the mobs and drug-running and so on, for me to make a good enough lie for them to believe I was telling the truth.

So they put me back in the vice.

I don't want to say no more about it. I kept passing out, and when I came to, they start and I'd pass out and so on. Then the last time I came round I was in the back of a car between the two heavies, with a gun in my ribs. I knew I was going to die, but I was almost pleased. At least the torture was over.

Chapter Six

Are you thinking what I thought for a moment in the car? A guy makes a perfectly ordinary but important decision to go and have sexual relations with a woman—O.K., O.K. so she's Candy Starr the film goddess, but what the hell, she's still just a woman, ain't she and he goes home to pack his stuff and the landlord makes him work five weeks to pay his debts. Well O.K., fair enough one time, but now he's paid the debt, he's in the cab on the way to the gates of paradise and boom, he sees the woman in the street and next thing you know he's gotten a crushed finger and he's <u>not</u> on the way to the gates of paradise, he's on the way to the <u>real</u> gates of paradise, because he's gonna be shot. And he's not gonna see Candy for the <u>second</u> time. WHAT THE FUCK IS GOING ON HERE, is it a punishment, is there a god after all, was momma right I shouldn't have gone with the wrong crowd after all like she said. WHAT THE FUCK IS GOING ON. WHO'S GOT IT IN FOR ME!?

One of the amazing things about life is the way you make friends and then lose them, the way you can make a very good friend fast and keep him for a long time, or make a good friend slowly and then lose them suddenly, and you don't know why, unless you really think about it, which I didn't usually take any time to do.

There was a guy lived in our street a few doors down who came from a very religious family, and he was a bit what the kids call a geek now, I guess, we used to call it straight. He went to the same school as me, and he was very good at lessons, and he was a pretty quiet, respectable type, and though I didn't go with the wildest gang, I thought he was pretty boring. And so did most of the other kids, so he was alone a lot, and he wore glasses and that kind of stuff. Then I started to get interested in girls and movie stars and having all those feelings that hit you like a wave from nowhere, and I didn't have nobody to talk about them with, because I felt no-one grown up around me would understand me, certainly not the priest that you was supposed to talk to about this stuff and somehow I started to talk to this boy, whose name was Antonio Marinelli.

Of course I didn't let on to nobody that I was seeing this guy on the quiet, and when I passed him in the company of my people, I was the loudest to rib him about his work and his glasses and going to mass or whatever. But when we used to meet, we could really talk, and he never mentioned the ribbing, which I think he understood the reasons for. And we'd talk about sex and god and teachers and sex, and I found out that his brother was a carpenter in the movies, and that impressed me quite a lot, and I used to pump him about what he knew about Hollywood, and I think he liked to be with me because he didn't feel so outside of things and I could tell him about the rougher side of things and so on.

Now this Antonio had what I suppose you could call a philosophy of life, which is pretty good for a young kid, but then he was pretty bright. And his philosophy went something like this. He saw life stretching out in front of him like a lot of paths, and you could sort of decide which path you took, and if you took the right path you could make something out of your life that was worthwhile and meaningful and you could really get ahead and nobody had to be a nobody. But the other paths were very near, at your elbow sort of, and if you only took the smallest step off your path onto one of the other paths, which might be a dangerous or harmful path, you could lose complete control and slide down to disaster and never get back to your first path, because there were forces on these other paths which wouldn't let you.

"Take this example," he used to say. "Supposing a happily married man decides to go with a woman of ill repute." (I laughed inside, "He means a whore," I thought but I didn't interrupt him). "So he goes to her house", (the guy thought whores had houses he must'uve heard talk of whore-houses), "and he goes to bed with her. So he's left his path for another one, right. Now he doesn't know that a friend of his wife has seen him enter the whore's house."

"How come his wife's friend is in the red-light district, if he supposed to be so respectable," I said.

"That's not the point," he said, "this is just a hypothetical example." See what I mean. Bright.

"Now of course he never intended the friend of his wife to see him enter the whore's house . . . ."

"Damn right," say I.

". . . . but she has, and she goes and tells the wife. So she is a force on the new path he has taken, which is out of his control. And the man's wife is very grieved . . ."

"What?"

". . . grieved, upset."

"Oh, pissed, right, naturally."

". . . . and she divorces him, and the children are very unhappy, and maybe the man kills himself or at least he feels very lost for a long time. And all this happens because the man takes just a little step off his path, just one little step. He probably doesn't even know he's off the path, and then terrible disaster follows."

Of course, all this was just really the ten commandments and hell and the church without him actually saying so, but it felt different to me then the way he said it and I don't think he knew either, and I used to turn the talk to examples of film stars going off their path, to get things moving in the direction that interested me, and he'd examine my examples and show me if I didn't fully understand it all, and we used to chew things over pretty much like that for quite a few hours for a few months.

Then I got serious about a girl and it took up a lot of my time, and we didn't see each other, and I haven't thought about him for twenty years until now in the car between the two heavies. Because now I knew what he meant. I'm not saying he was right, but I sure knew what he meant.

"Take this example," he could'uve said. "Supposing an ordinary guy decides to have sexual intercourse with Candy Starr. and he thinks he sees her in the street and follows her, but Candy's friend knows the man who got him her address, (which is the force on the new path which is out of his control), and fears for his life, then disaster could follow."

Antonio lived alone with his mother. If only his father hadn't gone to that house of ill repute. If only I hadn't decided to fuck Candy . . . .

As my head cleared slowly in the car, I thought bits and pieces of things. Why were we driving back to New York, why not kill me at the house? I could make a jump for it and knock the gun out of the man's hand. How come I felt like my normal self after going through the terrible vice? I could smash the window and shout. Could I talk them out of it, maybe with money?

I just sat. I felt dead already. That's how they do it.

It was night. I looked at the lights of cars of people who'd stayed on their original paths. I looked at the people walking their original paths. I looked at the houses of people who'd saved and worked to own their houses and stayed on their original paths. One of the torturers gave me a cigarette, which I smoked with my other hand. He lit it for me, very polite. They say a man sees the whole of his life pass before him when he's going to die. It's true. I saw my mother lean over and put a plate in front of me. I saw my father slowly sink into the chair after work. I saw my sister the first time with lipstick. And the hospital, the fan-club, Mexico, my mother again, the church, the priest, my first serious girl-friend. I started to cry again. The heavy pressed the gun harder into my side.

The only thing I didn't think about was Candy Starr.

The car stopped in the darkness, and as they pushed me out, I thought I could see we were next to a warehouse. The heavy with the gun stepped back from me. He could see me in the lights of the car. My mind flashed; a last wish, is it a dream, does it hurt? Then a voice called out, "Don't move, police, drop the gun." The heavy whipped round and someone shot him. The other two put up their hands. One called out, "OK don't shoot." I passed out.

I woke up a couple of times in a room. Each time I passed out again. Then I woke up for longer and there was a nurse looking at me, and I was in a hospital bed, and a cop was sitting in a chair near the end of my bed. The nurse looked at me and saw that I could see her, and she said, "Hello, Joe." "Hello," I said. The cop got up and came to have a look.

"Hi there fella, how's it going?"

"OK" I said.

The nurse looked at the cop and then back at me.

"You rest now Joe, everything's alright now."

She went away and the cop sat down. I looked around the room with my eyes and saw the white walls, a table, a window, some equipment and the cop looking at me. I felt calm and drowsy, I guess they'd given me some drug or sedative. But something was bothering me I hadn't thought about in the car. Had Chris known that Jimenez was a drug dealer, had he sent me up there for some awful joke, was that why he was laughing on the phone? I didn't think he had from what I knew of the guy, that wasn't how he got his kicks, and I knew he quite liked me. But it was possible, after all Jimenez had known him. I turned it over in my mind. Suddenly I realised that he couldn't have. If he had known Jimenez, he'd have known what he might do to me, and if it ever came out, it might also come out that he'd sent me up there. Jimenez might sing to get back at him. Chris wouldn't risk that. He was dumb, but not stupid. I felt better and went to sleep again.

Next morning when I woke, there was a doctor there with the nurse. The cop was still in his chair. The doctor had on his sympathetic face I'd seen round the hospital so many times.

"How are you, Mr Andretti?"

"OK," I said.

"Mr Andretti, I'm afraid we have some bad news for you. We had to take the finger off. There was nothing we could do."

"That's OK doc, I understand."

You'd think I would be upset about it, but I wasn't. Candy, Jimenez, the finger, they were all somewhere else. I was just here in the hospital, lying in a bed. I was passive. "Mr Andretti, the Iraqis have launched a nuclear attack." "That's OK doc, I understand."

"I'm glad you're taking it that way, Joe. You can manage with what you've got left." And he smiled. I realised he was making some kind of a crack about sex. Had he found out about me a Candy?

I looked down at my hand, which was completely hidden in a bandage. I remembered seeing the dripping red mess in the car . . . . They both went out. I lay there. I can't remember what I thought about. I ate lunch with my left hand.

That afternoon there was a knock on the door. The cop opened it and in walked Jimenez's girlfriend which I thought was Candy and a short-haired guy with a raincoat and his hands in his pocket.

I screamed at the cop, "It's them, they've come to get me," and jumped out of bed. And he smiled. HE SMILED! I saw his mouth open to say something, and the short-haired guy's hand started to come out of his coat pocket, and I ducked and ran out of the room, screaming, and my mind was saying. 'The cop's with them, he's one of them, he's with them,' and I was pretty weak and kept falling down and getting up and running weaving down the corridor screaming, and I nearly crashed into a trolley, and porters and nurses were looking at me and turning, and I heard people running after me, and next time I fell someone helped me up and held me, and a porter took the other side, and I was screaming and struggling and then my doc came running up, and over his shoulder I could see Jimenez's woman and my cop running over.

My doc said, "It's alright, Mr Andretti . . ."

"IT'S THEM, THAT'S THEM, THEY'VE COME TO KILL ME, THEY'VE COME TO FINISH IT!!" And I grabbed a nurse and held her in front of me, and the doc said,

"They're police, it's alright, they're F.B.I.

"I KNOW, HE'S WITH THEM, HE'S ONE OF THEM, HE'S ON THEIR SIDE!"

And the raincoat was quite close and had something in his hand which I thought was a gun, and I tried to kick it, but I was held too firm, and then I saw it was a wallet with a badge in it, and the doc was shouting, "CALM DOWN. THEY'RE F.B.I., MR ANDRETTI, IT'S ALRIGHT." And the raincoat said, "F.B.I., Joe."

"But she was there, that one, the one that looks like Candy, she was with him, she's with him, . . ."

"She's with us, Joe. She works for the Bureau. She was under cover."

And I looked at the raincoat and at my doc and at the woman, who really looked quite a lot like Candy. And I passed out again.

And I woke up again in my room, and they were all standing round. The raincoat takes my left hand and sort of shakes it.

"John Bear, F.B.I. For real, Joe."

I looked at my doc again to check.

"They really are, Mr Andretti. They're genuine." He turned to the raincoat and said, "Not too long, Mr Bear, please," and went out again with the nurse and the sister this time. I looked at the woman from Jimenez's place.

"This is agent Birmingham, Joe," says agent Bear and agent Birmingham said hello.

"She saved your life, Joe. She heard where they were taking you and got to a phone and that's how the police picked you up."

She saved my life. Wonderful. Thank you very much, I'm very grateful to you, agent Birmingham, thank you for bothering to dial a number and actually remembering which number to phone, and actually phoning and "WHY THE FUCK DIDN'T YOU STOP THEM SQUEEZING MY FINGER, WHY DIDN'T YOU STOP THAT, WHY DIDN'T YOU HELP MY FINGER, DID IT INTERRUPT YOUR SURVEILLANCE, IS THAT IT, DID IT, IS THAT WHY YOU DIDN'T?" I shouted, and started crying again.

She had a very low voice, almost as low as a man, but she spoke quite softly. she looked sorry, anyway.

"I'm really sorry about that Mr Andretti, but I was with Jimenez and I didn't know what they were doing to you. I thought they'd just rough you up. I didn't see you again 'til afterwards when I heard Jimenez tell them where to take you, and that's when I saw your finger. I'm really sorry. I haven't been with them long. I don't know how they operate totally yet."

Terrific. On our money they send dumb classy women who don't know what the fuck they're doing to spy on crazy murderers to protect the citizens. What could I say?

"Well fuck you," I said.

"She really couldn't have helped you," said the raincoat, "but we're really sorry. You caught us by surprise."

"I hope I didn't upset any important government business."

"I know how you must feel, Mr Andretti, but this man is wanted for a number of serious offences over a number of years, so we'd like to ask you a few things if you don't mind. It won't take long, I promise you. The doc says it's O.K., if we don't take too long"

Now I was really scared. I knew what they wanted from me. They wanted me to be a witness against Jimenez. Oh wonderful, oh fantastic, just what a nine-fingered man like me needed. I'd get protection 'til the trial and after my sensational revelations, which a dozen reporters would put in their papers and not worry about me at all, they'd take me to a plastic surgeon who'd stick my nose on the top of my head and give me three eyes, so no-one could recognise me, and then they'd send me to Mexico for me to start a new life, where I'd live in a paella and eat haciendas all my life among the goats and the pretty dark-eyed beauties.

In a pig's eye I would.

"Don't bother. I have nothing to say."

"Just a couple of minutes, Joe."

"And I won't go to court for you, either."

"Look, Joe, this man has killed a number of people, both directly and indirectly through his activities concerning drugs. This is our first real chance to nail this character. We just want to ask you a couple of things. You won't necessarily have to come to any trial. We'll see about that later. It may never come to that. Who can say?"

('Don't talk about my ma like that you fucking . . .' Bang!)

"I'm not talking."

"Joe, look . . ."

"If you don't piss off, I'm calling the doctor."

"Joe, it's just a matter . . . ."

"Nurse, nurse!"

The raincoat looked at agent Birmingham.

And he says, "OK Joe, we'll leave it 'til another time." They left.

And they didn't come back the next day or the day after or the day after, all the time I was in hospital, which wasn't long. I was happy, but I wasn't impressed. They'd come. Sooner or later they'd come. Their psychiatrists would pick the best time and they'd come. But I wasn't worried about it. In fact I wasn't too worried about anything. I thought about Jimenez, if they'd nail him without me, I thought about Candy and going to see her, I thought about paying the comedian and the jolly green giant. But somehow I wasn't in the middle of my thoughts. I couldn't grasp hold of any of them I couldn't really decide anything.

They took the bandage off my finger, and I thought about drinking my coffee with my thumb and third finger, but I couldn't even look into that very far. "Lucky you don't play the piano," the doc said.

So they checked to see I hadn't lost my marbles because of my experience, and sent me home.

I didn't go straight back to work. They told me at the personnel office to have a couple of days off. My job was there for me, but they thought that I should relax for a bit. They were pretty decent about it. So I lay around on the bed in my room, and went out walking and looking around, and went to a couple of Candy's movies. Two days after I got home, the landlord came up to my room.

"I haven't seen you round, Andretti. We getting worried about you."

"You'll get your money, don't worry."

I ain't worried. Where you been? Holiday?"

"I had an accident. I went to the hospital. They cut my finger off."

"I'm really sorry to hear that. What happened?"

"A Doberman dog bit it off. They took the dog away and killed it."

"Really? Hmmm . . . . That's really amazing. Did the dog eat the finger?"

Ugh.

"No, he was a vegetarian."

"Really? Very interesting. I guess that's why you shouted at my nephew and me last time, 'cos your finger was hurting, myself I don't like pain either."

And then the F.B.I. came round. And of course they sent over agent Birmingham. Brilliant. I can hear them discussing it now. "I think that considering he was chasing this film star and mistook Miss Birmingham for her, he's obviously going to be more willing to agree to what she says than if one of us goes over there. What do you think, Mr Bear?" See what I mean? Brilliant. Don't let me hear anyone complaining about their taxes, your money is being well spent.

Agent Birmingham sat in the chair. Her legs stopped somewhere just below her shoulders.

"How are you feeling now, Mr Andretti?"

"Lighter."

"I beg your pardon?"

"I don't weigh as much."

"That's probably just the natural reaction of your nervous system to the experience you went through."

"I meant I was lighter because . . . forget it."

She looked round the room at the pictures to which she compared quite favourably.

"I must say, I've never seen a room decorated like this."

(They told her, ". . . and don't start talking about the case as soon as you get there. Start with some casual conversation. Ease into it." Brilliant. How can ordinary folk keep up?)

"Very interesting."

"Yes, it is," she said.

"No, I meant it's very interesting that you haven't seen a room like this before."

"I'm sorry?" Money well spent.

"That's O.K."

"Have you been able to return to work yet?" she says.

"No. But I've taken up a hobby."

"What's that, Mr Andretti?"

"Finger-painting."

She didn't say nothing and uncrossed her legs and crossed them over the other way. For a minute I was afraid she might dislocate her neck. She was embarrassed.

"Well you certainly are very interested in Candy Starr, aren't you?"

"And how is everyone down at the fan-club?"

"I don't understand you."

"I thought you might have been intelligence-gathering down there, that's all."

87

"Have you been able to think about what Mr Bear asked you?"

End the easing-in part. Now we lean on him, legs, tits, mouth, everything is brought to bear on the poor dumb bastard.

"Not really. I've been too busy. I have this idea for getting energy from the bodies of F.B.I. agents." She smiled, bringing her smile to bear on the poor dumb bastard.

"Oh really? What's that, Mr Andretti?"

"You make 'em work for a living." Smile retreats.

"You don't like the police very much, do you?"

"Let me put it this way to you, agent Birmingham. No."

"Why not?"

"Because I don't want to live in Mexico with my nose attached to the top of my head for the rest of my life.

"I beg your pardon?"

"That's alright."

If she said 'I beg your pardon' again, I'd have to stuff her down the toilet.

"Why don't you like the police though, Mr Andretti?" (Because seriously, I seriously want to talk to you seriously about the things you think and feel and say seriously, and I've put on my serious face, or rather my face which shows I'm taking you seriously, so that I can find a way through to you and then a weakness and then GRAB YOUR BALLS AND DRAG YOU INTO COURT BY THEM.)

"It would take too long to explain."

"I have lots of time, Mr Andretti." J Edgar Hoover would have been proud. You know, with the slight suggestion there, that if you're a good boy, maybe afterwards, who know, if you play your cards right . . . It made me sick. She was like prostitute. Cunt for court.

"Why don't you go jump out of an aeroplane, and survey things on the way down."

"Mr Andretti," (low voice, very stern, very serious) "do you like crime?"

"Not even when the police commit it."

"Then are you aware what this man has done? Do you know the misery he has brought to thousands of people, often young people, by his activities? The people who have died, the prostitution, sometimes with thirteen year-old girls, the happy and respectable homes that have been ruined by his drugs? Have you any conception of the misery this man has caused?"

(Appeal to his better nature, they told her. He's probably a Catholic, so he's probably got a better nature. Appeal to it.)

"Agent Birmingham, do you like bull-shit?"

"No."

"Then are you aware what bull-shit has done? Do you know the misery bull-shit has brought to millions of people, often young people, by its activities? People have died of bull-shit, even thirteen year old girls, its ruined happy, respectable homes."

"What the fuck are you talking about, Andretti"

Ah ha. Either she was starting to snap, which meant she was human, or she was trying to come on strong, which meant she was still wasting her time. Later I found out which.

"It's simple, agent Birmingham. Even you can understand it. The story goes like this. Once upon a time there were some bad people and the police. And the police catch the bad people and put them in jail and all you decent folk are quite safe because the nice police are protecting you. And crime doesn't pay. That's the bullshit, with a capital shit. The truth is that half the cops are crooked, and the only difference between them and the bad people in the story is that you can recognise the police 'cos they got uniforms, and half the crime wouldn't be able to get done if it wasn't for the police, and crime does pay, and it pays about 4000 dollars a month to an individual police operative in this area of New York where we're sitting now. And as far as I am concerned, you couldn't protect me from a bird shitting in my eye, and you might not even want to, because your boss could be as thick with Jimenez as a tit and a bra-cup, and deals within deals and wheels within wheels, and maybe I should be more scared of you than I am of Jimenez, and that's why you're not getting me in court. I'm just one of those guys who doesn't believe it at the end of every episode of that old cop series that what's his face cleaned up the rackets single-handed. Sorry."

And agent Birmingham looked at me and she was really angry. She was practically spitting out of every pore in her skin. She stood up beautiful. I don't know if she was angry because I wouldn't come across, or just because of what I'd said, but she was really pissed with me.

"We haven't arrested this criminal for the good of our health, Mr Andretti, we're going to nail him, and you're our witness along with me, and we're going to get you to court whether you like it or not. We'll look into your past, we'll find ways if we have to. And you'll be protected whether you like it or not. Our best men are doing that around this building at this very moment and are in danger of their lives, and they're honest and straight, hard-working men."

And she walked out fast, unkissed, unfelt, unfucked. It was a new experience for me.

And the next day she came back, and amazing things happened.

Chapter Seven

I always thought that professional people like doctors and priests and police and lawyers were doctors and priests and police and lawyers all the time. When you met them in their office or they were in bed with their wife, they were always the same through and through. You know, like the old story about the professor who's giving a talk about Buddhism, and he says, "The Buddhists believe the world is supported on the shoulders of a giant." And this lady puts up her hand and asks, "What do the Buddhists believe the giant is supported on?" And the guy says, "I'm coming to that madam. The Buddhists believe the giant is supported by a turtle." And she asks again, "And what do the Buddhists believe the turtle is supported by, professor?" And he says, "I'm coming to that, madam. The Buddhists believe the turtle is supported by an elephant." "And what do the Buddhists believe . . . ?" "I'm coming to that. They believe the elephant is supported by a rock." "And what do . . . ?" "I'm coming to that. They believe that the rock is supported by another rock". "And what . . . ?" And by this time the professor is really pissed off with this woman, and he gives her a dirty look and shouts up to her. "Lady, it's rock all the way down!!"

Well, I thought this professional type of person was rock all the way down.

And I was wrong. And I first found out in the hospital.

We had a fellow working in paediatrics, which means kids medicine, and he was quite a snooty sort of type from Boston, and he was about thirty years old and a very good doctor, they said. And everything about this guy was doctor, like with all of them as far as I could see. He'd say good morning like he was writing you out a prescription. I never heard him talk about himself, nor what he did with anybody else, and I saw his wife come for him once in the entrance of the hospital, and he didn't kiss her, and he smiled at her like he was comforting her about the results of a cancer smear.

Then once he was working in kids' intensive care. Now kids' intensive care is a terrible hell on earth. You have kids in there who have eaten a live wire, and they're shocked and their mouths and faces are burnt right across. You have the boiling water cases in differing degrees of burns, with some kids looking like burnt meat off a spit, blown up to twice their size. You have the pneumonia cases, swallowing poison, accidents playing in the road, everything, cancers, everything. Everything you get in the adult wards, but it's kids. And the oxygen tents, and the drips, and the pipes leading into their throats. It looks like a Frankenstein laboratory in the movies, because some of them really look like monsters, they've been so deformed. And the parents grey in the face, weeping and crying, and the kids screaming and calling out for help sometimes. I tell you, so help me god, so help me Jesus, it's enough to break your heart. A place of pain.

And suddenly we hear that this doctor has taken a leap out of his tenth floor apartment, and of course is dead. And after the rumours have died down from the people who said he was having affairs and all of that shit, it turns out it was as simple as it seemed. He couldn't stand the pain of the kids. And even more, telling the parents and relatives when the poor little things had died. It just got to him, it broke him up and he died. And I hate to tell you this, but I liked the guy better for it, but of course I was just a little on the late side. Maybe if I'd known and had a talk to him about it . . . . ? You know how you feel after those things.

And it made me feel different about the doctors and nurse, and even a little about priests and lawyers. But the police I still felt they were rock all the way.

But I was wrong again, and I was soon to find out.

So the next day very late, about eleven o'clock at night, there's a knock on my door, and it's agent Birmingham looking even more like Candy by the artificial light.

"May I come in, please," she says, "this is not an official visit."

In a beautiful police-woman pig's eye it ain't, I thought.

"You come to give me all-night protection?"

"Well no. I . . . it's . . . I came to apologise for what I said at the end of our talk yesterday."

Now I knew it was official. You know, the old corny thing, where one of them bangs you while the other talks to you nice and reasonable like Spencer Tracy in 'Guess

Who's Coming To Dinner?' And she was playing both parts. The holy police duality. Tonight she was Spencer Tracy. (Yesterday Dick Tracy.)

"Well this is very kind of you, agent Birmingham, because I was very upset after out little talk, and I cried all night and this morning I wrote my mother."

She smiled and sat down with her bag hanging over her crossed knees, in which there could have been a tape recorder.

"Anyway, I'm really sorry for what I said at the end. I know how you must feel about being involved with these kind of people."

And I said, "Thanks a lot," and waited for the next manoeuvre, and there wasn't none. She just sat there and started to look real embarrassed and kept looking at me as if she was hoping I'd say something and then she'd blink and cough and look around, and either she was as good an actress as Candy, or she was really not at ease, and I started to have a teeny little doubt. I didn't let it get too big, but it began. But I wouldn't show it.

"Game of cards?" I said.

"I'm not very good, I'm afraid," she replies. And then more of the 'I-don't-know-what-to-say-at-this-point' type acting. Or real . . . .

I started to get a little embarrassed myself. The thing was confusing, it didn't fit.

"Well, aren't you going to ask me questions?"

"I told you Mr Andretti, this is not official, It really isn't."

"Well what are you here for then? Oh yeah, the apology. Thanks. Thanks for the apology. You'd better go now."

She said. "Oh," and didn't move. She just sat there and said, "Oh," and the "Oh" and her face said, "Going is not what I had in mind." And a little bell rang in my head, and instinct and habit came into play and I said "Would you like us to make love together?" and she said "Thank you, Joe, I'd like that very much." And she stood up and started to undo the button on her dress, which was a kind of pretty expensive suit, and she was undoing the buttons of the jacket and smiling at me. When she got to her bra and pants, she stopped.

"I won't take these off. Some men like to do it themselves," she said.

You know the story of the two bulls? The young bull gallops up to the old one and says all out of breath, "Hey man, there's a bunch of beautiful cows in the next field. Why don't we smash down there and grab one each and fuck 'em." The old bull finishes his mouthful of grass and says, "I'll tell you what we'll do. When I've finished this beefburger, we'll <u>walk</u> down and fuck 'em all." Right?

Now the young bulls amongst you will say to me, "Jesus, man, now you <u>know</u> she's giving you the big come-on, just to get you into that court hassle. You was wise to that already, so why don't you throw her down the stairs?" And the old bulls will reply, "Joe, she may be offering herself as an inducement to get you to give evidence, and she may not. But so what? I suggest you accept her offer of sexual intercourse and <u>then</u> throw her down the stairs." I am going to follow the advice of the old bulls.

Women and men express their personalities when they make love. That's well known, nothing special about that. And what Janet expressed, (I found out she was called Janet during the course of the intercourse.

She said it was a turn-off when I said "I love your ass, agent Birmingham," and laughed), what she expressed was calm. It was the calm of an expensive education, of horse-riding, of a chauffeur, of big rooms with a lot of space between the arm-chairs, and tennis courts behind the pool behind the lawn behind the patio. And when I say calm, I don't mean she was passive. We made love all over the room, on the floor, against the walls, on every piece of furniture. She lay on her back with her knees apart and her legs hanging over the table, while I licked her from her toes to her ears and she massaged her breasts with the spit from my mouth. Her breasts were swollen in her bra and pointed slightly out from her body. Her hips, which were narrower than Candy's like I'd seen, shuddered like a horse's side again and again. She gave and gave and took and took. Her body was like a present she made to me, always something different, in a different shape, wrapping and unwrapping, and then accepting my thanks opened out like a smile. And she told me what she liked. "I like it when you lick my neck. I like it when you press my arms together behind my back to kiss my breasts. I like it when you spit in my mouth." And when I did what she liked, she thanked me like a nun for charity. And she remembered my injured hand. All the way through, in the middle of her pleasure, she remembered it. When she twisted my arms behind me, to sit on my defenseless mouth, she hurt my arms, but gentle with my hand. It wasn't love-making, it was love. And we finished lying on our sides on the floor, looking into each other's eyes, with Candy squashed under our bodies, and looking down at us from the ceiling. We were like two spare-ribs, welded together by the fire, greasy, sweet-smelling, you would have to tear us from the bone to separate us. And I knew she was telling the truth. It was not an official visit. She was not rock all the way down. And no-one was kicking anyone down no stairs.

"Jesus."

"Joe."

I don't know how long we looked at each other.

"What's the bureau going to say?"

"They'll be very angry. I may lose my job." She may lose her job for Joe Andretti, hospital porter.

"What happened to you, Janet, for Christ's sake?" She knew what I meant.

"It was in the hospital, when you were crying and shouting at me, and then you told Bear in the middle of it, that you hoped you weren't holding up any government business. It was like a flower growing through concrete."

"Yeah but, but . . . ."

Why was I but-butting? It was simple. In a complicated world, it was so simple. She had a square daddy, a square mommy, a square school, square boy-friends, square college and now square associates like the raincoat. And then she met the dispenser of the anti-concrete neutron bomb, which smashes concrete, but leaves flowers alive, and she was twenty-five years hungry for him. I'm not being swell-headed. That's what I was to her. And you know what she was to me. I just told you.

"But . . . but that was just a gag. I was just being sarcastic."

"But I was right though, wasn't I? I was right about what it meant, wasn't I?"

Yeah. She was right. In the middle of her pleasure, she had remembered my hand. She was right.

We lay on the bed together. She told me her father was a lawyer, police work seemed interesting and important, they had asked her to take the exams for the F.B.I., she passed them easy, did I like Mozart, how often did I go to the club before I freaked. Jesus, I know it sounds corny, but to us it was Adam asking Eve about apples.

We lay there talking, licking each other like horses lick foals on nature programmes. Then we went to sleep. In the morning, we woke to the buzz of an alarm in her wrist watch. But she had set it an hour early, so we gave love again, this time very gentle, thank you—thank you for ever—for ever. Then she got up and got dressed and went to work for the greatest happiness for the greatest number of people.

Chapter Eight

"Hey, have you heard, Joe Andretti isn't going to fuck Candy Starr, he's going out with an F.B.I. agent!" "WHAT!" "Yeah, that's right, an F.B.I. fucking agent." "He's . . . he's . . . ha ha ha. Ha ha ha ha. Ha ha ha ha ha HA HA HA HA HA HA HA HA HA HA HA HA HAAAAAAH!" "Hey, Andretti's fucking the F.B.I!" "Have you heard about the F.B.I. They're fucking Andretti!" "Ha ha ha ha ha ha ha ha ha . . . ." "Hey . . . ." "Ha ha ha ha." "Have you heard . . . ?" "I know, it's incredible, remember when he used to always say 'Fuck the F.B.I?, ha, ha, ha, ha, ha!"

It <u>was</u> incredible.

'Good evening. Here is the news from C.N.N. The hospitals of New York are receiving an influx of patients of epidemic proportions, people suffering from hernias, burst blood vessels, heart attacks, and other ailments associated with severe strain. Though in considerable pain in some cases, the patients all enter hospital laughing hysterically. Doctors are seeking the source of the outbreak, and speak of an unknown virus. Our reporter went to the house of one of the laughers who, when questioned, replied, "Andretti's fucking the F.B.I," and then fell down four flights of stairs into the street and died. He was laughing.'

Who could I tell? Family, friends, people at work? I didn't even tell Mike at the hospital. They'd have all died laughing. Who wants to kill their friends?

But why should I care if I couldn't tell nobody? I had Janet. She licked me like a horse licks a foal in the nature programmes.

Janet did have a lot of trouble about me at work. They were very angry about how she couldn't get me to testify, and about how it had worked out between us after that. She said they would have fired her, if they didn't need her so much. And they had to let Jimenez go. Her evidence alone wasn't enough. That meant Jimenez might come for me. I hardly even thought about it. Janet licked me like a horse licks a foal on the nature programmes.

Of course we didn't have no cosy, home-by-the-fire kind of relationship. Janet was working. I went back to work, her work often took her out of town, or she would be out 'til all hours. When we went out, people used to stare at her, some just because she was beautiful, some because they thought she was Candy Starr walking around with a nobody. Some people used to ask her for her autograph. We used to laugh and I'd lick her neck, which made her face colour and her eyes stand out as she got turned on, and she'd look at me, staring through my eyes into my thoughts, right there in the street in front of the autograph hunters, with promises in her face which she always used to keep when we got home. We'd go to the movies, for walks, eat out, sometimes she'd take me to a bit of culture, but she'd never push it. She wasn't trying to educate me, get me up to standard for her parents and such bull-shit. I didn't care anyway. Mostly I'd just look at her enjoying the culture. I figured I had all the culture in the world anyway in her. And we used to talk. About us. I used to rib her about being a cop, for instance, and she'd interrogate me.

"Mr Andretti, if that's your real name, which we have means to ascertain, what were you doing on the night of the 23rd?"

"I was balling an F.B.I. agent."

"Right. And anyway we knew that from our undercover people. Obstructing an officer in the course of her duty. That's a ten stretch. I produce the following item as evidence of the crime, and ask the court to label it Exhibit one."

And she'd pull out my dick, and you can guess how that finished up.

And we talked about the hospital, and she'd tell me about the case she was working on, which she wasn't supposed to do, and of course, we talked about our previous relationships.

"You know the trouble with you, Andretti? The trouble with you is you're sex mad."

"Me sex mad? ME sex mad? You sit there, the Lucretia Borgia of the law enforcement agencies, and tell me that I'm sex mad?"

"That's right."

"Listen, Lucretia, you didn't learn what you know from no book learning, you know."

"Any previous sexual experiences I may have entered into were simply a preparation to ensure a successful consummation with the man of my life, when I found him," said very snooty, with her head in the air.

"Oh I see. You just fucked half a million guys as part of your post-graduate education programme."

"That is correct."

"Well let me tell you, lady, I am just a normal, healthy, ex-Catholic boy from the lower East Side."

"I'm glad you reminded me, Andretti, I will now hear your confession." And she'd sit up and pretend to be an eighty year old sex-starved priest, rubbing her hands and licking her lips. "And tell me the dirty bits, Andretti. Only the dirty bits."

"Well father, I did sin just a teeny bit last week, but it wasn't my fault. I'm completely innocent . . ."

"I don't want to know about you being innocent, Andretti, you disgusting pervert, I want the dirty bits." And she'd rub her hands some more, and we'd break up laughing.

"Well father, it's the McGinty sisters. I slept with them all on Friday morning."

"How many sisters are there, my son?"

"Eighteen, father." She'd be laughing so much, she could hardly sit up.

"Tell me, tell me."

"Well, Nancy McGinty decided to take her dress off because she was too hot.

"Show me, show me, strip, strip, show me!"

And you can guess how that finished up.

After about two weeks, I pretty much moved in with her into her apartment, though I didn't drop my own room. Also, Janet paid the rent I owed to the landlord. So we went on like that for a couple of months. And then one day I woke up and I wanted to go and fuck Candy Starr.

Right. You're surprised, right? You thought, 'The guy has everything he wants, what does he want this for again?' And you're a bit angry too, because maybe I've got a bit more than you anyway, and you figure I ought to be grateful.

Well I was surprised too. I was more than surprised, I was very surprised and I was guilty about Janet and I didn't understand it either, so I thought about it and this is what I come up with which may not be what it is, but it's all I know, anyways.

Going with Candy Starr was like a dream. It was like wanting something special in my life, something important, something perfect and I must'uve always wanted it, but it only came out at the club on the neutron bomb day and since then it don't go away. Maybe it's something about me being a good Catholic boy, (or more a bad one,) maybe it's the American dream which I hate, but all I know is I have to do it with Candy to make my life special before I die even though I got Janet and I have to and that's it.

So now I had a problem. One, do I tell Janet and go, two, do I not tell Janet and go, three, do I not go. Well I was going, so it was one, because I had to tell. That was the relationship.

She took it great. First thing, she laughed.

"Andretti, you're crazy and I love you."

"Are you very upset, sweetheart?"

"What are you talking about? That's how I met you in the first place."

"That's true," I said, and I was feeling really low and guilty, "but maybe having you ought to stop wanting to go and do it with her again."

She was making coffee, and she stopped and came over and picked my chin up and made me look at her.

"Andretti, I love you. I've arrived, and the place I've arrived at is you, and that means I take whatever comes with the main course. So stop feeling badly about it."

And she kissed me with her tongue and went back to the coffee. "And if you go on feeling badly about it, you can always go and see somebody."

I said, "What do you mean, see somebody?"

"I mean get some professional help. It may be something we can't solve by ourselves."

"What do you mean, 'solve'? So there is a problem."

"Not for me. But you're upset about it, and if you stay that way, that would be a problem."

"But I'm only upset because I'm scared you might be upset. But if you're not, there's no problem."

"That's right, darling."

"You mean see a doctor. A shrink."

"For instance."

"So you think I'm crazy. Like everybody else."

She came over again and smoothed my hair and my forehead.

"Joe Andretti the first, my love and my happiness, you work in a hospital, and you know as well as I do that people seek help for all kinds of things, like sex problems, marriage problems, help with their children, and none of them are crazy, so stop making waves when the weather is so good."

"But those people have a problem with a relationship. But you said you're not jealous."

"I'm not."

"Then we have no problem. So why should I go?"

"Only if it stays a problem for you, darling."

"But it only stays a problem for me, because I can't believe you're not jealous. How can I know that? How can you prove it?"

And she took her clothes off and gave me her love, not proving anything, not pushy, not trying to cover up something, to drown my worry in my pleasure, but like at first, like always, calm, for-ever, for-ever. And of course it did prove it. What other proof could she give? She could see I wasn't satisfied with her words, so she did what no jealous person could do, she gave herself to me without trying to prove anything. And I knew it was true.

"I believe you," I said. And a minute later, "And how do I know you don't think I'm crazy?" So I didn't believe her. And she laughed under me.

"You're just greedy, Andretti. Anyway, I don't go to bed with crazy men."

"But you'd like me to go, wouldn't you?"

"If you ask me for a yes or no, I'd have to say yes." Which gave me the creeps.

It gave me the creeps, because I knew she wasn't jealous and I knew she didn't think I was crazy, but it was like there was a third thing which she didn't know and so couldn't tell me, like from those science-fiction films, where the enemy is beaming something into your brain from a planet in space, and you don't even know it's happening. Because she had to have a reason for wanting me to go to a shrink and she said the reason was me, but I was only upset because of her, because she had to have a reason for wanting me to go. And round and round and round.

"You want me to go and get cured."

"I don't know if you'll be cured, whatever that is, as long as you aren't upset about it any more."

And then I thought it might be some stupid reason, like she cared what other people thought, (though she didn't know it), but that would have meant she <u>did</u> think I was crazy. And round and round.

And then <u>I</u> started to have doubts. Maybe I <u>was</u> crazy, although I knew I wasn't. Like some of the fruit cakes in the psychiatric wing of the hospital who thought they weren't crazy. One part of their brain just didn't tell the other part that anything was wrong, and some of them were going round the ward thinking they were a lettuce leaf and thought you were going to drown them in mayonnaise.

WHY (pause), DID SHE WANT ME TO GO TO A SHRINK, (pause), IF SHE DIDN'T CARE ABOUT CANDY, (pause), AND SHE DIDN'T CARE IF I GOT CURED, (pause), AND I WASN'T UPSET, (pause), UNLESS SHE WAS, (pause). WHICH SHE WASN'T, (pause), EXCEPT I WAS UPSET, (pause), BECAUSE SHE DID WANT ME TO GO, (pause), ALTHOUGH SHE WASN'T UPSET.

I went on like that for about a week. Janet took it very calm. She never got angry with me, she never got irritated.

Right. OK. Cut through the crap. I could either tell her to fuck off, or I could go and see the shrink.

So the maid opened the door of this large house on the Upper East Side, 67th Street, and showed me into the waiting-room, which was big enough to take a 747, and I nearly suffocated in the cushions of the chair I sat in. Then another door opened and the shrink asked me in, and I sat down opposite him across a desk so big, I thought I'd have to shout to get him to hear me. I sat in a wooden chair, he sat in a soft, foam upholstered swivel job, so he could look out of the window. He was a young guy, thirty acting thirty-seven, tall, good-looking, with gold rims on his glasses and a moustache, and hair which was respectable but fashionable. You know, wavy but cool. To show you he read all the latest theories and was about as up to the minute as a three hundred dollars could buy you anywhere in the city. But the big thing about him was that he was obviously sharp and he could obviously help you. That's not from what he said, as you will see, but he spent the whole hour just beaming out at you that he was obviously sharp and that he could obviously help you. Because you <u>MATTERED</u>.

Without being prejudiced after only seeing him for about one and a half seconds, and trying to be as objective as I could, I thought he was a prick. So you can see how hostile I was right from the start. But he changed all that. By the end, I knew he was a prick.

"Good afternoon, Mr Andretti. What can I do for you?" OK, fair enough.

"Well doc, to be honest, I'm not exactly sure."

"That's fine. That's alright. Let me put it this way. What is it that has brought you here?"

I was going to say, "The subway," but I decided I'd give him the benefit of the doubt at the off. Give the guy a chance, we used to say, if we caught one of the other gang alone, out in the open. Then we'd chase him off with stones.

"As I said, doc, I don't exactly know."

"I see, that's fine. Let me ask you this then. What is the problem?"

"That's it, I don't know if I have a problem."

He smiled. "Oh, you have a problem alright."

Shit. The guy was a genius. He must be a clairvoyant. He could see into my brain. I felt like my flies were undone.

"Oh, you know I have a problem."

"Yes, I do."

"How do you know?"

"Because you've come to see me. Mr Andretti."

"WHAT!"

"Why does that upset you, Mr Andretti?"

"Supposing some guy comes in, and it turns out he doesn't have a problem. What then?"

"Then he thought he had a problem, and that's his problem."

Catch 22. Brilliant, if you've got a problem, you've got a problem, if you ain't got a problem, you've got a problem. He'd had his chance. I started picking up stones to chase him off.

"Supposing the window cleaner comes"

"He comes to clean the window."

"Supposing your mother comes to see you." I knew she had a problem. A prick for a son.

"Then she's probably making a social call."

"But if someone comes to see you professionally, then he's got a problem."

"I would say so."

"You got it made, right."

"In what way would you say that 'I've got it made'."

"Listen, the cops need evidence to make you a crook. At least mostly. A priest'll at least wait to hear your confession before he'll call you a sinner. But you're in business it's right away."

"Shall we return to your reason for coming here, Mr Andretti?"

"I haven't got a reason for coming. I came because my girl wanted me to."

"Yes?"

"Yes." Make the bastard work. Who did he think he was, the F.B.I.?

"And why did she feel she wanted you to come?"

"I don't know. But it's something to do with me wanting to fuck Candy Starr."

"Is she jealous about that?"

"No."

"But she thinks it's strange."

"No. I don't know."

"Do you know Ms. Starr?"

"Not personally."

"From films, and so on."

"That's right."

"And how do you feel about this desire you have?"

"Very strongly."

He smiled. "I mean what do you think about it?"

"Nothing much."

"Do you feel guilty about it?"

"No."

"Do you think this desire is unusual?"

"No. Most men have it"

"You mean you think many men want sexual intercourse with Ms. Starr?"

"I guess lots think they do. I don't know how many really want to do it."

"So you regard this feeling you have as perfectly normal."

"Yes." I felt I was going down. I answered very flat and low. I felt there was danger coming up from inside of me.

"I see. That's fine. How long have you felt this desire?"

"A few weeks really wanting to do it."

"And why haven't you gone ahead with it?"

"A few things came up."

"What kind of things do you mean?"

"Back rent, an accident, Janet."

"But when these practical things are out of the way, you fully intend to carry out your plan or purpose, shall we say?"

"That's right."

"I see. Fine." He swivelled in his chair to the window and wiped the corners of his mouth with his thumb and first finger.

"Do you think it's normal?" I said.

He swivelled back, smiling that he could obviously help me and that he was obviously sharp and that I MATTERED.

"I don't know enough about you to answer that question yet. Mr Andretti."

I swallowed. "But it might not be?"

"It might not indeed. On the other hand it well be"

I had the idea of slicing his head across the top from ear to ear with a razor, and putting my fingers into the cut and pulling his skin down over his face, down to his neck. While he was choking on the blood, I was digging about in the muscles in his face and leaning with my fist on his teeth one at a time, hearing each one crack off in turn. I wanted to tell him, but then I knew he'd think I was crazy. I had to prove I was normal. It's easy to prove you're not guilty. You get witnesses. Have you ever tried to prove you weren't crazy? Somewhere in my head I knew I could leave, but it didn't happen. Everyone needs redemption, the priest used to say.

I put on a normal smile.

"Would you think I was crazy if I was a film producer who wanted to make it with Miss Starr?"

"That would depend on the precise circumstances."

"Well would you think I was crazy if I was Miss Starr's husband?"

"He would be unlikely to come and see me about that, I think."

"So it's just because I don't know Miss Starr that might mean I was crazy?"

"Some people might regard it as unusual." Like him.

"Winston Churchill was unusual, wouldn't you say, doc?"

"I never examined him. Mr Andretti."

I was sweating in my hands and on my forehead, but I didn't want to wipe it away, in case he didn't think it was normal. I hoped my hair was covering the sweat. Then he asked me a lot about me and Janet, about our sexual life mostly. I answered normally, showing what a regular guy I was. I didn't say anything about meeting her because I chased her thinking she was Candy.

Then he started asking me about my parents, mostly about my mother and if I liked her, and how I felt about her. After half an hour, I felt a bit calmer.

"Well doc, am I nuts?"

"I think you would benefit from some treatment." I was nuts.

"Think you can cure me, doc?"

"I think I could be of some help to you and your young lady."

I told him I couldn't pay his kind of money, so he told me he could arrange some group therapy for me three times a week at a hospital for free. I told him I'd think about it.

"Nothing to worry about, Mr Andretti," he said. I thought about getting Chris to give <u>him</u> something to worry about. "Thanks a million, doc, I feel better just talking to you about it."

I thought about burning his house down, or putting sugar in his gas-tank, but I didn't. Group therapy three times a week meant <u>another</u> reason I couldn't see Candy, maybe for months, maybe a year. But if I didn't go what would Janet say? I felt very tired inside when I thought about Janet and the shrink. I'd just go and see Candy. The two of them would just have to think what they thought. I'd be far away, anyway. Maybe that was my problem anyway, I was thinking too much about what people were thinking, so fuck 'em really this time. This time I was just going.

When I got to the apartment, my sister was waiting outside. (The sister I caught masturbating, who threw me out of her house when I brought it up). We hadn't spoken for three years, there was only one reason she could be here.

Money.

I saw a cab parked a little ways down the street outside the house when I took my sister inside.

Chapter Nine

I didn't hate my sister, but I didn't like her either. I guess we just took two of Antonio Marinelli's different paths. Her path was the path of righteousness, and mine was the path to Candy's front door. She was two years older than me, so we weren't that close as young kids anyway, and when we grew up. I thought she was the primmest little bitch this side of Doris Day. My ma didn't help, because she kept saying, 'Why don't you do like your sister? Look at your sister, she don't get into no trouble,' and things like that. And she used to snitch on me too. 'Mama, Joe's torn his new shirt; mama, Joe said fuck again, mama, Joe said Sophia Loren's got a big ass.' Of course, I used to get back at her. Put rats in her dresses, little things like that. When she started having monthlies and growing tits, I started to get quite interested in her, and wanted to discuss it with her, but she pretended nothing was happening, though you could see she knew something was happening, because she used to walk around with her head in the air, so she couldn't see her body walking around underneath her. One of the older members of the gang started dating her, but it only got as far as drinking ice-cream sodas. When he put his hand on her tit one day, she slapped his face, and told him not to be dirty. Word got around to the fast workers in the neighbourhood pretty quick, and she was left alone to continue on the path of being pure.

Except, of course, when I caught her with her finger in her snatch.

She married a guy who owned a shoe store, (the shoe business, he called it), and they had a couple of children and went to mass a lot. I used to go and see her sometimes, at first with mama, then to get a meal, if I had nothing better to do. Then came the incident with mentioning the finger in the snatch, and I hadn't been there since, because she didn't want my kind of people corrupting her children, etc.

I led the way through Janet's apartment, and she sat down. She had on a pretty dress with flowers on it, and seeing her again after a few years she was quite an attractive woman. Her tits had grown too.

"This is a very nice apartment, Joe. Have you got a better job?" Shoe salesman, maybe?

"No. I'm sharing."

"Oh."

She didn't dare ask with who, in case it was with a woman and I was FUCKING HER.

"Is work alright, Joe?" I just wanted her to come out with and tell me how much she needed, and go and let me pack and go and see Candy. I wanted to leave before Janet came back, if I could.

"Work's fine."

"The children are fine too, and Peter sends his love." I will make you a fisher of shoes. "And mama sends her love too."

"Sophia, I'm in a hurry, there's something I have to do. What did you come for?"

"I didn't come for anything, Joe. I just came to see you. Can't I just come to see my brother?"

She must want a lot of bread off me. I went and made a cup of coffee. She talked through to the kitchen.

"So work is O.K., huh Joe?" I'd have to let her get there in her own time.

"Yeah."

"And everything else is O.K. too?"

"Yeah."

"Not married yet, naughty boy."

But I'm doing a lot of FUCKING and DICKING with the PRICK in the CUNT and the TIT in the MOUTH.

"Never know."

"Anybody in mind?"

Yeah. I had someone in mind. And on my ceiling and walls and floor, too. She'd seen my place. She was disgusted.

"How did you find me?" I asked.

"I phoned the hospital, after I went to your room." I brought in the coffee. Her little finger stuck out straight when she drank. She noticed my finger was missing.

"Joe, what happened!?"

"Accident."

She ran over and began soothing the finger with purity. She didn't like a brother with a finger missing. As if it wasn't bad enough me FUCKING people with my PRICK. Now there was an amputated finger. It was messy, imperfect.

"Joe, how terrible. How did it happen?"

"Priest bit it off in confession."

"Joe!"

"Happened at work."

How awful, how terrible, how frightful, how dreadful, could I still work, could I still manage, could I still live. Eventually we got passed the finger drama. It was probably a punishment for my sins, anyway, right?

"So how's Peter? The business O.K. Making plenty of money?"

"Things are a bit slow now, with the economic situation. But it'll pick up again soon, God willing."

"So everything's fine."

"I can't complain."

"So what have you come for?"

She got up and walked around with her arms folded across her middle.

"I hate to bother you, Joe, and I know we didn't always agree about things, but there's no one else that can help me. You're the only person, Joe. I talked it over with mama." She was getting out the big guns. 'I talked it over with mama' meant that there was no way out. This is how it was going to be.

"What's the matter?"

"I'm pregnant."

"So? Congratulations. So?"

"I can't have the baby."

"So get rid of it." It was a bad joke. She was totally against abortion.

"Mama wants me to go to the best clinic."

"WHAT! You're going to get rid of it? Mama agrees? What's going on?"

"I have to."

"Well what's wrong? Does Peter want to keep it?"

"No."

"Well what's the problem, are you sick?"

She looked at me, and I get there just before she said it.

"It ain't Peter's baby."

Ah ha ha ha. Ha ha ha ha ha ha ha. HA HA HA HA HA HA HA HA. I was having hysterics. This was perfect. This was beautiful. The Virgin Mary was fooling around. The Pope was queer. God was dead. Bull-shit oh bull-shit, thy name is bull-shit. My sister had a body after all.

"Joe, please."

"What happened? Who was it? How many times? I want to know. I have to know everything."

"I don't see why that matters."

"Oh please. Oh now please, dear sister, I have a right to know. You want me to pay for an abortion, (she jumped because I guessed before she asked), you want me to lie to my brother-in-law, the shoe fetishist . . . ."

"He is not a shoe . . . ."

". . . . you want me to be a party to a mortal sin, at least I have a right to know what I'm getting into here. I could burn in hell for this, you know."

She started to cry. The wages of sin is a new life. I thought her tits were on the big side. I tried to stop laughing.

"I don't see why you have to know what happened exactly," she wept.

"No story, no bread."

"You are a bastard. I should never have come here."

I was loving it. Better than putting rats in her dresses any day of the week.

"Well, what's the story, sis? . . . ."

"Well . . . . Peter and I haven't been . . . . close . . . . er . . . for quite a while . . . and . . ."

"So he'd know the kid wasn't his."

"YES!!!" She screamed it.

"So? . . . ."

"I met someone. We only did it once!" More crying. (". . . and supposing this woman meets a man of ill-repute, she will fall from her path . . ." Marinelli for president).

"Where did you meet him?"

"He came with his daughter to the Sunday school."

I sat back in my chair.

"Well, well, well." Well, well, well. Come back, gang. Put your hand back on my sister's tit. It ain't that she don't like it, she's just a bit kinky. She doesn't like it in an alley. You have to do it to her in church.

"Well, well, well. There are seven million stories in the naked city. How much do you need?"

"I still need seven hundred dollars."

"What! I haven't got that kind of dough." Nor did Janet at that moment.

"Couldn't you borrow it? Couldn't you get it somehow, couldn't you get some more at work? Please, Joe."

I went spare.

"Oh, I see. You want me to work my ass off to pay for your pathetic fun and games in the wife-swapping belt. You go fuck yourself. Or the Sunday school teacher or whoever. You think I'm going to slave to save your rotten bull-shit marriage? Forget it. What about the father of this sexy affair? Why doesn't he pay for his moment of weakness?"

"He's given what he can, he hasn't got much."

"Well nor have I, baby, so you can forget that straight off."

"Joe, please, you've got to help. I'll kill myself. I can't stand it."

I was just going to tell her a couple of good, clean ways to commit suicide, from my experience in the hospital, when the bell rang.

It was my mother.

"I hear you quarrelling downstairs in the car." Four flights down, with the windows closed, she hears us quarrelling in the taxi. "Come in, mama." A seventy year-old woman at the key-hole, hearing the sins of her children. She sat down. Sophie was still crying. Mama didn't look at her. "Well?"

"I haven't got seven hundred dollars, mama."

"Six hundred, seventy-eight."

"I don't have it. What's got into you anyway, mama?"

My mother was a tall, lean woman, with a handsome face, even at seventy. She worked three times as hard as my father, who worked his ass off, and never complained once in her life. And she could do anything. She cooked, she sewed, she made clothes for us, she painted the apartment every three years, she washed, she ironed, she fixed chairs if they broke, she made carpets, curtains, toys, dolls, and she grew tomatoes in window-boxes. She was busy every minute of the day, and she was happy. She was generous with her time to friends, she cooked for neighbours who were sick, she made baby clothes for Sophie's kids, and when we were kids she had time to have fun with us, to take us to fair-grounds, to the circus, to the theatre. She loved her husband and her children, and we felt it.

But.

That wasn't what mattered to mama. What mattered to mama was God. Maybe that's why she was so relaxed about her life. Because she knew it wasn't real. But God was real. He was Italian, Catholic, had a regular job, and when I was a kid, I thought he must be grand-father Andretti, (who was dead), because according to mama, the way she spoke about them both. God always wanted things the way grandfather Andretti wanted them. 'Grand-father Andretti would turn in his grave, grandfather Andretti would never allow, grand-father Andretti would never say,' and God always thought pretty much the same way. The only time I ever remember mama really being upset was when the priest told her that I had lost my faith. She didn't say a word, but she went to bed for two days. When she got up, she didn't scream and shout like some of my pals mas, but she spent the next six years trying to get me to go out with religious boys, and religious girls when I got older, pushing gently but firmly for me to finish up at the right hand of grand-father Andretti in heaven.

And though I asked what had gotten into her, really I knew. Either it would come out that my sister had committed adultery, or she had to help my sister commit an even greater sin, which is abortion, and save the family and the family name. I guess she thought God and grand-father Andretti cared more about the family name.

So you see, what mattered to my mother wasn't God, it was what people thought. And I knew that from way back. And that is where I got my collection of anti-bullshit neutron bombs.

"Joseph, I only ask because there is no other way."

"Do you know what you're doing, mama, this is an abortion we're talking about, you know that, don't you?"

"Think of your nephews without a father." And think of what people will say about <u>why</u> they haven't got a father.

"Then she shouldn't have frigged around." Not a word against my language

"But she has." (You should not have stolen the radio, my son. But I have. Bang!)

"Then let her take what's coming to her, if she can't get out of it herself."

"But must the whole family suffer, my son, because you will not help?"

"It ain't because I won't help. I just don't have that kind of money, mama."

"You could work for it, my son."

"Jesus Christ, ma, do you know how long it would take me to save that much?"

"Your father will die of a broken heart."

That was it. That was finally and truly the bitter fucking end. My sister was going to kill herself and my father would die of grief, and it was my FAULT! Not hers. Mine. Not her fault for flaunting her cunt around the kid's Sunday school, but mine, because I was a no-good, lazy, ungodly . . . . I was blazing. I released my anti-the whole fucking world neutron bomb right into my mother's face and I didn't care, first the land-lord, then the drug barons torture me, then Janet makes me fall in love with her and then tells me I'm crazy, then the shrink wants to hold me back and now my mother, my own frigging mother wants to bury me as well, like in the dream, just like in the frigging dream, the whole frigging world was trying to stop me getting to Candy, there was a conspiracy by the whole world to cover me and my dream in grey concrete and stop me getting my share of happiness, well I blew the mega-mega-megaton bomb right up in their fucking faces.

"You can forget it, mama, I mean it, you can just forget it. And you. Sophie, you can just go back home and put it out of your mind. I have something else I have to do, which I have put off long enough, and I'm not going to that fucking hospital and slaving the shit out of me for the sake of the opinions of a few clapped-out, fucked-up, bull-shit minded neighbours, and not even if the Pope hears about it and excommunicates the whole fucking family, you hear me. And if you want to know, you've got a fucking lot of gall coming here to me with this, mama, if you want to know, do you know that? For thirty years you're preaching to me to behave myself and be a good boy and have pure thoughts and deeds and this creep is ass-crawling around you with her high and mighty halo on her head, greasing up you and the teachers and the priest, and winning all the prizes, and I've got a pair of horns and a fucking tail with a hook on the end of it, and now, when this little whore shows what's been in her mind all the time, you both wander over here, cool as cucumber, and ask me to bail her out of hell and save the family honour, when you wouldn't have asked me my opinion about what to have for lunch two weeks ago. Supposing it's bad money, eh mama? Supposing I live off women, mama, would you still take the money? You bet your ass you would. And Jesus would stuff it in his wallet and thank his daddy for Christian charity. You bet he would. Take your daughter and go, mama. Maybe the new kid'll be nice to you and keep you in your old age.

My mother stood up, and she was shaking like an epileptic. She was full of hatred for me, and I for her. Anti-bull-shit neutron bombs do that to people.

"If you do not give the money, you will never see me or your father again in this world."

I bawled out, "I AM GOING TO FUCK CANDY STARR THE MOVIE ACTRESS, YOU HEAR ME, I AM GOING TO FUCK HER AND NOTHING IS GOING TO STOP ME ON THIS EARTH. THAT HYPOCRITE OVER THERE CAN HAVE HER FUN, AND I HAVE TO DROP MINE? FORGET IT, NEVER!!

And the voice of god and grand-father Andretti which is greater by far than all the neutron bombs in history put together thundered out of my mother's mouth. "First the money, <u>then</u> you fuck the star!."

Chapter Ten

So I was back doing overtime again.

What? You thought after the big scene I'd just pack my bags and leave 'em holding the foetus? Listen, it's only in movies that the hero tells his elders and betters to drop dead, and then goes and gets to be chairman of the world bank. But not in life. In life he just <u>tells</u> them he's going to be chairman of the world bank.

It was ratting on the family that got to me. A catholic boy has it deep in his head you can't rat on your family no matter what, even though I hated Sophia and my mother for what they was doing to me once again, when it came to deciding to go to Candy I couldn't rat on these close family people. Give me a child for the first seven years of its life, right?

I often used to watch the Oprah Winfrey Show. I didn't like the ones where she drools over big stars, but the ones about human relations and problems in the family and so on I learned a lot from and I used to like. And there was a shrink on once (pushing his latest book how to shrink yourself as well,) and he said if you could see a pattern in your life it was probably you was causing it, not the other people you was blaming all along. Was the land-lord my fault? And the finger and the rest of it? And now I was doing what mama wanted and putting Candy off again. Was it a pattern, was it me doing all of this to myself, putting off going to see Candy? I put the pattern thing out of my mind the second it came in there. Screw the Oprah shrink, it <u>was</u> them, it was fate not me, screw the shrink.

So I was doing the overtime and I was in a rage. I was in a rage twenty-four hours a day, seven days a week. At the hospital I dropped things, I broke things, I crashed into things. I was like Woody Woodpecker boring through concrete to get away from the cat. I was taking time and piling it up behind me like a hero of the Soviet Union piles up mountains of coal to meet his production target. I was Moses splitting the waves. I didn't speak, and when I had to, I shouted. I told Mike to fuck off when he tried to be nice, and nurses used to walk the other way when they saw me coming down a corridor. I nearly killed two patients with neglect. They would have fired me, but I think they were too scared and anyway experienced people were scarce.

At home, when Janet had asked me about the shrink, I told her to mind her own god-damn business. I didn't care what she thought, or what people thought, I just wanted to get that six-hundred and seventy-eight dollars and throw it at my sister and GO. Janet took it like always. She was kind and good, and waited for me to come back to her with my feelings, but I hardly noticed, and anyway, I was hardly ever there. I told her she had to let me have whatever money she had, and I didn't thank her, but it helped a little to the target.

And all the time, I was planning in my head. I'd been a fool. I should have had a plan. With a plan, you don't get stopped, you don't get turned away from your goal. With a plan, I said, you can even beat your own patterns (if there is a pattern.) I worked out a fool-proof plan, and lost ten pounds in weight.

The plan was to make sure I didn't get side-tracked. I didn't go to the movies, even when I had the time, in case I could meet someone I knew and get into something, some diversion or whatever. I ate alone in the canteen. I never volunteered for nothing.

I was seven weeks keeping myself pure and separate like that, like a girl for a Hindu wedding.

When I had the money, I took it to my sister. When she opened the door, I shoved it in her hand and said, "Here," and went.

When I got home, I took a shower, had something to eat, and put the Plan into operation.

I phoned the airport to check the flight to L.A. next week. Was it flying? Were there any possible changes of schedule? I would check again later in the week. I phoned the union representative at the airport. Were they putting in for better wages? Was there a chance of a strike? Was there a chance of a strike in any department in the airport. I phoned the service section. Did they have any problems about fuel, or any other problems. I phoned the security section about hi-jack problems and and bombs and what they was doing about it. I said I was a newspaper reporter. I booked a rail ticket as a back-up. I booked a bus-ticket as a back-up to the back-up. And did they have any problems. I phoned the weather bureau about landing and take-off situations in New York and L.A. I phoned the cab companies. Everybody happy? I phoned city hall about parades, foreign presidents and kings and road-work. I worked out routes for the cab. Three alternatives. I worked out everything. I checked everything.

Then 'phoned Candy's agent (which we knew at the club). I said I was the director of her last picture, which I knew who he was too, and said that I had to see Candy about certain cuts the distributors was asking for, and see how that squared with her contract. I'd spoken to her lawyer about it, he thought I ought to check with her personally. Was she home on such a day, was she away filming, could I be sure of getting her? They bought it, yes, she was home, did I want them to make a time to see her? No thank you, that won't be necessary, I'd do it myself, and by the way, my secretary had become schizophrenic and burnt all my files, could they remind me of the address and phone number. Certainly, Mr Big-shot, she so enjoyed working on the picture with you, etc. And please be sure and not speak to her about all this, I might be able to sort it out without bothering her. I put switched off the phone. If they did check about the call, or mention it to her or her lawyer, they'd just think it was some fruit. What did I care, I had what I wanted to know and I was on my way.

The whole thing took four days. I covered every angle.

I re-checked everything over the week-end, and walked around the apartment like a relation waiting for bad news at the hospital. Tomorrow was the day.

I got up, put on a sharp check jacket, slacks, shirt and tie, packed a few things for a longer stay. I looked in the mirror. I had thick, black hair, good face, tall, in good shape, nine fingers. Not bad. "Hello, Candy," I practiced, "I've come to make love with you. I've waited a long time."

I left a note for Janet that I would be gone, maybe for a long time, I hoped I'd be back, etc., etc., etc . . . Of course she knew where I was going anyway.

The cab didn't need none of my special routes. There were no parades, road-ups, traffic-jams, bomb-scares. The plan was working. I got off at the airport and walked to the departure lounge. I felt very friendly to the other passengers walking around. I smiled at one or two, who smiled back, not knowing why. I checked in. The girl told me I still had half an hour 'til my flight. I bought a magazine and drank a cup of coffee. Ten minutes to go, I went to the john. I saw myself looking sharp in the mirror. I took out my prick to piss in the bowl. Almost nothing came out, just a slow dribble, and it was very painful, sore and burning. I recognised the pain. I knew the symptoms from the hospital and from some previous experience of my own. It was non-specific urethritis.

V.D.

Chapter Eleven

I remember the last time I really cried.

I was sixteen, and I was in love with a pretty girl with long, blonde hair, who looked like a young Debbie Harry. She didn't go to the same school as me, but I used to pass her on the way home. We got talking and we got walking and we got necking, and I was deeply in love, and knew the meaning of happiness and the meaning of pain. Happiness was necking, and pain was not necking. It got round to going to each other's homes and going out in the evening, though not too late, because grand-father Andretti wouldn't have liked it, (though he'd been dead twenty years even then). It didn't get round to sex though, because she was keeping herself for me for when we got married, which I always hoped would be next week. But it was getting close. (Sex I mean.) She used to allow me to put my hand into her bra and I had got her as far as rubbing the outside of my pants.

Then holidays came, and she was going with her family to stay with an aunt who lived a hundred miles out of town. My mother agreed to let me go for two weeks, and it was all arranged between the families. I said good-bye to her at the station, and she gave me a poem, and I swore to remain faithful for the ten days before I saw her again at the aunt's. When I got there, her parents was very nice to me, and so was the aunt, and I was walking around in a haze of love and sexual frustration. I started calling the parents ma and pa, and we all used to go for walks, and the girls used to go riding, which I didn't do, but I watched her ass bumping up and down on the horse, and looked at the horse's cock. And we used to go for walks alone. We'd lie in a field and neck and I'd crush her under me and pull her on top of me, and try to make her take her clothes off. Both of our lips were getting sore and had little cuts in them, which her parents must have seen. One evening she got so turned on she took off her blouse and bra. She had beautiful breasts, very swollen and young and tight, and I kissed them and sucked them and bit them for an hour, we both had an orgasm from rubbing each other through our clothes.

That night after the orgasm, we was sitting holding hands on the floor in front of the fire, and I felt something was wrong. She wasn't talking. We had so much to talk about, about sex and school, and what we was going to do with our lives, and how many children she wanted, and how stupid our parents were, and now she was silent. When I asked her what was up, she didn't say nothing for a bit, and then she said that when I went home we shouldn't see each other again. I felt sick and asked why. And it turned out that her parents thought we was getting too close, what with me calling them ma and pa and the cut lips and everything, and they thought we shouldn't see each other for a few months. I cried a little and felt very betrayed because she was taking her parents side, and we'd even talked about running away together, and now she was throwing me away for the sake of stupid grown-ups who didn't understand young people like us. But she wouldn't change her mind, and I was so upset., I walked out of the house, and left my toothbrush and things there, and hitched back to New York, because I'd spent all my money and I wasn't going to ask her for any. In the truck on the way home, I felt beautifully sad. The whole thing was so tragic and romantic, and I sat next to the driver with my secret which I didn't tell him 'cos he wouldn't understand, and thought about her, how beautiful she was, and how I loved her more than anyone else in the world, and what a stupid seventeen year-old jerk she was for not letting me fuck her, and being to prim and proper and well-behaved and throwing away the only chance for happiness she'd ever get.

I got home early in the morning and walked past my mother, who didn't say a word, and went up to my room and lay on the bed and cried for three hours. I cried for the world and I cried for myself, and I cried for the stupidity of people who didn't understand, and I cried because I'd been rejected.

And I cried and cried and cried.

And now I went into a cubicle in the airport john, and I sat down and I cried and cried and cried. I heard people outside discussing what to do, and one guy put his head over the top and asked me if I was alright but I went on crying and took no notice. And as I was crying I thought, 'I know I could just go ahead, because you can still fuck someone if you've got V.D., and she'd never know, and I could make sure she went for a check at the hospital, and non-specific ain't life-threatening or nothing,' but I knew I couldn't do it because it was not perfection to fuck Candy Starr when you know you've got V.D..

And the reason I was crying was because no-one was stopping me going except me this time. No-one was holding me back like with the other things, the debts and Sophia's abortion dough and everything. I could walk and talk and fuck with V.D., but something in me was telling me I couldn't go. I argued with it, I wrestled with it, but in the end I knew I couldn't fuck my Candy with V.D. And I hated myself for my weakness, for my morals, for my scruples, and I hated the world and my mother and grand-father Andretti for what they'd had done to me.

And the other reason I was crying was because I knew now that I never would get to fuck Candy. I knew I'd never get up the courage again, I'd never get the drive, the hope, the certainty. I was beaten. They'd won. Bull-shit had won.

And I cried for my youth and for my hopes and for the things that would not be, and like in the car with the heavies next to me, I saw my life pass before me, because I felt that I was going to die.

And in a way I did.

I went back to Janet and I went back to work. Janet had read the note. She never said nothing about it. When I told her to go get a check-up, she never questioned me. She was kind and gentle. She fed me and held me close, trying to warm life back into me, but there was no way. She never asked why I didn't go, she never asked why I came back. But there was no way to warm my broken heart.

At work I was the exact opposite to what I was before. I was slow. I forgot things. I forgot what people had told me. I was late. I was silent. Mike covered for me when he could. He told me to go and see one of the doctors for some tablets to help me. I didn't go. I didn't care.

And I went on the skids.

I started drinking heavy. I went to bars after work and sat alone, drinking one bourbon after the next, and staggered home to Janet. I didn't answer when people tried to talk to me. I walked past other drunks, past drug-addicts, I was sick in the gutter, I was sick in the side-walk, I was sick on the carpet at home. Janet cleaned up. Janet cleaned me up, put me to bed, got me up in the morning, made sure I had clean clothes for work. When she couldn't be home, I went to work late and dirty and unshaven. I was sick and I didn't care, and I didn't care I didn't care.

Slowly the blackest part passed. I started to say 'Hello' to people at work, I answered when Janet asked me what I wanted to watch on television, but I still drank. Except now I talked to the people in the bars. And I was deep in the land of bull-shit, and I was a citizen. 'Nixon was the biggest crook ever. They should'uve put him behind bars. They should'uve fried him. They should'uve shot him. They should'uve tortured him. Found out what else he knew. That was our money, you know, taxpayer's money he spent on all that cover-up.' Or, 'Nixon was the greatest President this country ever had. Great man. Great statesman. What about China? Stopped a nuclear war. Guaranteed. And started the fall of Russia' 'Yeah, but would you buy a second-hand tape from him? Ha ha.' 'Ford was a good man, but he never had a chance to show it.' 'Ford was a bum.' 'Carter was the man who could'uve put the economy back where it belongs. His election speeches were very sincere. And he was very religious, you know.' 'Carter was a bum.' 'Eisenhower is a bum.' 'Was a bum, you mean.' 'Excuse me, fella, I fought with Ike. He's a great man.' 'Was a great man, you mean.' 'Who asked you?' 'Well if you're talking about him being a general, I agree with you. But as President all I can say is he was a great general.' Ha ha. 'You think it was a plot?' 'Course it was a plot.' 'You don't think Oswald could have done in alone?' 'Course not. Look at the evidence. Look at the evidence, for Christ's sake.' 'Take it from me, friend, Truman had no choice. Absolutely none. He had to drop it.' 'Truman was a bum.' 'Reagan was a great president, he restored America's self-esteem.' 'Yeah, but I saw on television . . . . '

Experts. Lonely experts. Lonely drunken experts.

Or.

'Hi there, my name's Anthony.' 'Joe Andretti.' 'You married, Joe?' 'No.' 'What do you think of marriage, Joe?' 'It's O.K.' 'You wouldn't if it was my wife you was married to.'

Or.

'I just don't get it. They've got more money than I ever had when I was a kid. and all they can do is take drugs and mug old ladies and rape and blow up buildings we paid for. I'd put 'em in the army.'

Women, communism, sex, blacks, Cuba, terrorists, power black-outs, oil, energy, the ozone, Elizabeth Taylor, China, the deficit, we had all the answers. We thought we thought 'em up ourselves, but we was just throwing T.V. headlines at each other. Because I joined in. I was one of them. And I got to know a lot of them, because we were all regulars. When they found out I worked in a hospital, they called me 'Doc.' 'Hi, doc, found the cure for cancer yet?' I used to go home with some of them, to go on drinking there. And uptight wives used to pretend to make me welcome as we sat there drunkenly talking bull-shit. Because drinking dulls the pain, but you can still think. But talking bull-shit stops you thinking.

Sometimes I used to go to my room and cry a little at the pictures of Candy, and I'd be late to work again.

And I started going with prostitutes. I went to a club with one of the boys, and we'd dance and then go back with one. I remember the first one I slept with. She was a big, muscular girl, very good looking, black, and she wore short pants and boots. She had very long legs, and her thighs didn't taper down to her knees like most women, they were like torpedoes that curved into the knee at the last moment. When we danced she stuck her thigh into my crutch and pushed it up against my prick in time to the music, and all the time she was talking to her friend, who was dancing near us with someone else. "What does the cunt expect me to do about it? Sit round here on my fucking ass all night, while he gets it together? Suck him." She made love like a frozen statue, unless you paid her extra, and then she made love like a moving frozen statue. I missed Janet, but I didn't want her either at the same time.

And I got to know a lot of the whores like I got to know the boys. "Hi Joe, want some? Want some pussy tonight, Joe?"

And I went to the parties which were excuses for orgies. That's what they called them. This one I went to started with a woman there who was a medium asking everyone to sit round a table, and she'd get in touch with anyone we wanted to talk to from 'the other side'. I was pretty high and feeling friendly, which I didn't always, and I asked her to give a call to my grand-father Andretti. They turned off the lights and the woman went into a trance and started talking in a deep voice with an Italian accent.

"You want to talk to me, Joe?"

"Yeah. How's it going, grand-father Andretti?"

"Fine Joe. How's your mother?"

"Fine. How's grand-mother Andretti?"

"She's fine too. How is the hospital?"

"Great. We keep sending people up there to join you, grand-father Andretti."

"I know."

Next to me, a short woman with blonde permed hair and big breasts and thick glasses started to cry. I looked around the circle. The medium was a scrawny woman with her dress cut almost down to her waist and a lot of make-up. and a scar on her forehead. Next to her sat a fairy with grey hair and a bow-tie. There was a girl with lots of mascara and wearing a Red-Indian dress, a fat man, bald, in a light grey suit, a woman with asthma and a few others. And I was sitting there too, talking to God.

When the session was over, people started drinking and necking, and then taking their clothes off. I was in the arm-chair with the blonde with the sensitive soul. Whenever I touched her, she started to pant. I could see the Red-Indian girl over her shoulder, fucking the fairy with a dildo up his rear.

I had made it. I was with the liberated people. Liberated, freaky, lost, crazy people full of bull-shit. And I was one of 'em.

At another party I saw Chris and Hazel. He asked me how things were going, and if I'd made it with Candy. I just laughed. I didn't say nothing about Jimenez and nor did he. Later on Chris put on an exhibition where three chicks were sucking and chewing his prick, while Hazel sat on his face watching and telling them how he liked it. And all because his father used to shove him under the table and kick him.

I was under the table now. And I was kicking myself.

I was three months like that. Maybe to you it sounds that I met some very weird and interesting people. I don't think so. I think I was dead. I was down and out. I was going no-where. The only reason I didn't kill myself, was because it seemed too important a thing for the way I felt. My mind was all grey.

Chapter Twelve

One day I just got home to change to go out with some woman I'd met in a bar, when there was a ring on the bell. I called for Janet to open the door. That's the way things were, I was going out with some pick-up, she was staying loyal. A young guy came through, about twenty-six, very bright, very clean, very Martini shaken not stirred.

"Yeah?"

"Are you Mr Joe Andretti?"

"What do you want?"

"Joe. I'm Art Buchner. How do you do. May I have a minute?"

"Who are you? I don't know you."

"I work for . . ." He said some letters.

"Well I don't want nothing. I'm just going out . . . ." I went on dressing.

"We represent Candy Starr, Joe." I looked at him for the first time a little longer.

"So?"

"May I have that minute?"

He sits down in a chair anyway. I was still standing, buttoning my shirt.

"Nice place."

"Yeah, like a cathedral, what's this about?"

"We have an idea I think, that is we think, might interest you, Joe."

"How'd you get my address?"

"I followed you from the hospital."

"Why couldn't you talk at the hospital?"

I had some vague fears about Jimenez. I didn't know what and I didn't care too much either.

"Christ, Joe, you can't talk business at a frigging hospital."

And he laughed a couple of gold fillings.

"Well, what is it anyway?"

"Have you got a moment? You said you were going out."

"Well what is it anyway?"

"Right, O.K. Well Joe, it came to my notice, our notice that is, the agency's, through your local fan-club, that you were taking off to er . . . meet, you know, with Candy. Is that right? Can you confirm that?"

"Does she know about this?"

"Jesus Christ, no. We don't tell her about every freak who . . . that is, well not you, of course, but you can imagine the kind of things fans do and send and so on, of course. You must know that from the fan-club anyway"

"So?"

"Well, do you confirm the report we got?"

"Yeah. I was going to see her. I ain't now, but I was"

"Right, O.K., well as you know, Miss Starr has just finished a picture, and the agency thought that you might be interested in a project in connection with promoting her and the picture."

"Did the committee and the club put me up for this?"

"Jesus Christ, no. An individual 'phoned us and told us about you and then I suggested this to the highest meetings in the agency, Joe. Of course I'm not in a position to go into details about this whole deal, but I can tell you that it's quite a thing, and promises to be very big, as a matter of fact."

Yeah, like everything else in bull-shit land. Everything in bull-shit land promises to be very big.

"How do I know this is on the level and not some kind of creep's joke from the club or whatever?"

"Well you only have to phone our number tomorrow, and then, if you're satisfied, you can come in and see me, us that is, right away. You can come in any time tomorrow, as a matter of fact. We'll see you any time, which is fairly unusual for our agency, as you probably know."

He wouldn't tell me no more, so I said I might come up, and he made me promise that I definitely would, because that's why he'd been sent, he said, and then he went.

As he goes I asked him who the guy was who 'phoned him from the club.

"It was a woman, Joe, a Ms. Janet Birmingham, very generous gesture on her part as it turns out."

He didn't know how generous. Janet was seeing me drunk and down on myself and miserable and screwing other women, so she goes a round-about way to Candy's agency to make me happier. I was gonna cry there and then and I pushed the Martini man out the door.

I went into the kitchen and hugged Janet and fell on my knees in front of her crying and apologising. She lifts me up and we go into the living room and sit down holding each other, my head in her shoulder.

"I've been such an ass-hole, I'm sorry, I'm so sorry, sweet-heart." She just stroked me. "I don't know why I got so down about it, but being frustrated all them times and I guess it must mean something special to me more than it seems, 'cos I've just been feeling so bad and terrible, but that don't mean I should be down on you about it, I'm truly sorry." And I asked her about her V.D. check—up, but she was clear.

Later we discussed if I should go to the agency.

"If you want to, I think you should go, or else this'll just stay as unfinished business and you might go on feeling like you have been feeling for a long time."

"God, I don't know. I don't feel about Candy like I used to, but I guess something's still telling me to follow through."

So we agreed I'd go.

I wasn't that excited. I saw that it might mean that I'd see Candy, but I was coming to it from a long way back, like coming out of a quicksand, but I was only clear so far to my nose. So we sat around for the rest of the evening, 'course I forgot about my date. I wondered what it was all about. Well anyway, I'd see tomorrow. Janet and me went to bed at the same time for the first time for a long time. For the first time in a long time too, I read a newspaper.

I 'phoned in the morning, it was on the level. They'd be very pleased to see me whenever I could get in. I'd be seeing Mr Swain himself, and the girl sounded as if that was very special.

The agency took the whole floor of a block of offices. The carpet was like walking on a water bed, and the receptionist smiled at me as though she knew what it was all about, and treated me as if I mattered. I sat in some kind of molded plastic chair, and all the time Martini men and Martini girls went by, laughing and talking. After about five minutes a sort of Sharon Stone type walks over and says she's Mr Swain's personal assistant, and asked me to follow her. From the door of Swain's office I took a bus over to Swain's desk, and he shook hands with me and introduced me to his partner, Mr Baum. S. and B. Associates, that was the letters Buchner had told me. Son-of-a-Bitch Associates, almost. In the old days, I'd have laughed.

Swain was a tall man, about late fifties, grey hair and very sun-burnt, and I didn't like him at first. But when he got talking, he sounded pretty straight.

"Well Mr Andretti, what do you think of this crazy show-biz nonsense we've dreamed up for you?"

"I ain't sure I really understand it."

"Well, to be honest about it, we want to use you. You'll be well paid for your services, but the truth is we want to use you. Candy Starr has just made a movie, which is shortly to be released, and Art Buchner in our publicity department heard that you wanted to fuck Miss Starr for real and thought you could help her career and the film with a series of appearances and interviews in which you could say as much as you wanted about your feelings for Miss Starr, and why you feel as you do, and so on."

"Is this normal, you know, like O.K., I never heard about no-one doing this for Candy before."

"You're right to ask, Joe, this could be John Lennon country, right, so we checked your back-ground a little and everything's fine, just fine."

"I work, you know."

"Absolutely. And we have no intention of changing that, unless you wish to do so on your own initiative. In fact, we think that your whole story, from the point of view of its presentation in the media, will enhance what we are seeking to achieve if you do remain at work, because that would remove any element at all of eccentricity from your image, and present you as what you are, a normal, regular, average guy. If you agree with that assessment, we would arrange any and all engagements in the evening or at week-ends, to fit around your work schedules. How does that sound to you?"

"To be honest, I feel pretty uncomfortable about the whole thing at the moment."

"I think that's absolutely natural and to be expected, frankly. You arrive here from a solid life of work, and are thrown into the insubstantial, fluffy world of entertainment, which let's face it, Mr Andretti, is mostly bull-shit, and not only are you thrown into it, you are invited at a price to take part in our silly fun-and-games. I think you're bound to feel uncomfortable for a time. The only thing I can say, is that we'll endeavour to ease that problem by any means we can. As a first step towards that, please ask any questions at all that come to mind. Anything. Anything at all."

"Well what exactly do I do?"

"You won't <u>have</u> to do anything, of course. In fact, we've decided to draw up the contract in such a way that you can refuse at any stage to continue the campaign.

That's not only for your benefit, it's for our own protection too, of course. As far as what we'd like you do to, that's pretty straightforward. We would arrange some appearances on T.V. in talk shows and interviews with the press, and all you'd have to do would be to answer questions that they put to you. We'd prime them with the story, and it would just mean telling it in your own words, as they say. We'll start small, with a local station, then if the thing starts to roll, the media will contact you on their own initiative, and we'd simply make sure that there was nothing potentially harmful to you or us in their request, and then you'd go ahead as before. And that's it really. Of course we hope that the financial inducement we're going to offer, and the chance of meeting Miss Starr will keep you with us, but as I said, that's entirely up to you."

"So it's just talking about me and Candy, and so forth?"

"That's it. There may be some attendances at film premieres and eating out at night with a star or a newspaper columnist, but basically you've got it. It's telling your story."

"I don't have that kind of clothes, you know."

"A wardrobe and accessories would be part of our campaign expenses, and you mustn't think of it as charity or any such thing, you could keep the clothes afterwards, or return them to us, whichever."

"Sounds O.K. How much do I get?"

"A thousand dollars a week."

"Jesus!" I looked at Mr Baum. He looked pleased too.

"Well, Mr Andretti? Are we in business?"

"You must be if you're handing out that kind of dough!" He laughed pleasantly.

"Listen, I'm gonna check with my girl, O.K., but I guess it'll be O.K."

So I talked it over with Janet again. I could see she wanted to get the thing out of her life and though I wasn't screaming for it no more, I still wanted that special something and a grand a week wouldn't hurt either.

So I was in show-business.

The first thing was they got the wardrobe for me. After I had signed the contract. The contract seemed O.K. It read like Swain had said. We had to buy ready-to-wear, because they wanted to get going, but I ain't hard to fit, and pretty soon I had a few very sharp outfits. And shoes to match and everything. Going around with two of the Martini men shopping, talking about which suit would fit in at which hotel or for the Late Show, driving around in a big Lincoln, I was starting to believe it. It was happening, it was going to happen, I was going on T.V. and I was going to meet Candy sometime and I was getting a big bill every week.

And I started to love Janet again, which made her happy, though maybe she wasn't happy about me actually touching Candy's body, but she didn't say nothing and I didn't ask. She thought the contract was legally O.K. and she smiled when she saw me in my new clothes.

They decided to 'break the story' to T.V. first, and then the papers might follow. They got me on an afternoon chat show pretty quick.

So before the T.V. they asked me to come in and discuss my story with the 'image guys.'

"Hi Joe, sit down, won't you."

I was feeling pretty good. Looking good, feeling good.

"O.K., Joe, problem one is the word 'fuck', right. Now you're a pretty forthright type of person, which is good, because this is a forthright type of deal, which is what will interest people in you, and which has got us the first T.V. spot already, right. But fuck, cunt, prick, spunk, all that stuff has to go, right. It won't be accepted on T.V., they'll cut us off or cut it out and it might fuck the whole deal, if they think you're too vulgar, right. So the story is, you want to meet Candy, right. <u>Meet</u> her. Everyone'll know you want to fuck her. but we don't say so. You want to meet her, and if they press the point and ask you <u>why</u> you want to meet her, you just say because she's beautiful and sexy and a brilliant actress and you've always admired her, but never that you want her body, right."

"They'll think I'm a phoney."

"Joe <u>they'll</u> know you want to fuck her, <u>we'll</u> know, <u>you'll</u> know, everybody knows, but we can't <u>say</u> it. O.K., it's 2014 we know, but it's not the movies, this is T.V. which goes into folks' houses, right. No fuck, right."

"O.K."

"And the rest, right."

"O.K." After all, I wanted to meet her and fuck her with a few grand in my pocket. Should I blow it now, after what I'd been through? Like Futelli said, I would moderate my language.

"Second, right. The hospital. You work in a hospital. In a hospital you get bodies. You push bodies round, don't you?"

"Sure."

"Exactly, right. Dead bodies, naked bodies, old bodies, burnt bodies. You know bodies, you're an expert, you've seen it all, and there is only one body as far as you're concerned. Candy's, right. Now go easy on this thing. We don't want any sick notions about fucking dead corpses to creep into folks' minds. Mutilation, fetishism or anything.

147

But you know bodies, you are familiar with them, and you've made your choice, right. That's the angle."

"You just said never say I wanted her body."

"For Christ's sake. Joe, of course you don't say it. You hint, right. You suggest. You make links. It's sub-conscious, subliminal. You never say anything. You just let them think it. Jesus, for Christ's sake don't say, 'I've seen a lot of corpses in my time, and a lot of bodies, and I think Candy's is the best, dead or alive.' You hint, you imply, right?"

"O.K."

"Third, right. You're catholic. Sex is sin to Catholics. We don't want the Catholic Church on your back and we don't want the Religious Right and we want as little trouble as possible from the P.Cers and the feminists, and above all we don't want any unpleasantness rubbing off on Candy. So no childhood stories about the priest touching your buddy behind the altar and so on, right, the church, mass, everything catholic goes."

"It's O.K., it don't bother me anyway, I'm lapsed."

"That's right. Good . . . . what's lapsed. What's that?"

"Means I've left the church."

"Perfect. Beautiful. Right fourth. The business with Jimenez. It's beautiful, excellent. Call him by a different name if you're worried, but we keep it. Beautiful story, funny, ironic, shows how much you value Candy, found your girl-friend via this strange and dangerous escapade, oh yes, mention Janet, she's a cop, a regular guy, show the finger, no problem, perfect."

So we invented this story about Candy and me to tell the world, which 'cos it was half-true wasn't true. But I was going along for the ride.

And then it all started.

My first talk-show was a big success. It was run by a woman in the afternoon, and I told the story the Martini men and I had worked out, and I was very polite and all of that.

"But what do you think a huge star like Candy Starr and you will have to talk about when you meet her?"

"Well, she's a very intelligent woman and I'm sure she'll lead the way in the talking department and because she's sensitive and knows I'm just a working guy, she'll know like where to pitch the thing anyways, so I'm pretty confident we'll have plenty to talk about."

The image Martinis were wild about it after—'sensitive, intelligent, lead the way' I got in, I was better than their advertising people, they said.

Bull-shit, bull-shit, thy name is bull-shit.

"And you don't feel intimidated at the thought of spending time with such a world-famous figure?"

And I gave her some more nonsense that was acceptable to the Polite People.

After the show, the woman said she thought the interview had gone off O.K. and I see her look at me pretty respectful and more so than before we started. Then some local papers picked it up, and I had a lot of interviews, and there were fashion magazines and film magazines, and I had my picture in all these papers and magazines, and a couple of the reporters were women, and one of them was very women's liberation and didn't like what she thought I was all about, but I just told her straight what I meant and that to me Candy was a person and very special, and she just had to swallow it, though her article wasn't too complimentary.

The other woman reporter was very glamorous and she asked me out, but I said no, because I was too busy.

Later I did the Late Show after all and another one, and I met a couple of stars and personalities, and we had drinks at the studio before each show, and they were pretty polite.

Then a guy wanted to write a book about me, but the agency weren't interested, so I let it go, and another guy wanted to write a film script about my life, but the agency said he just after a porn-movie angle after they talked to him, so I let that go too. People started to recognise me in the street and ask for my autograph. Of course it was mostly women and girls, and some of them came on very strong and asked me out and told me their husbands weren't any good no more, and some were very crude and asked if they could suck me off and stuff like that.

But I never met Candy.

Swain arranged a dinner date for me and Candy's permanent movie stand-in, and laid on photographers, and the next day there were articles in the papers about me looking glum because I hadn't met the real thing and 'Joe Andretti makes the best of second best,' and stuff but though I'd asked quite a few people in the agency by now, I <u>still</u> hadn't met Candy.

So I decided to go back to Swain and have a little show-biz show-down, 'cos Joe Andretti was coming back to life a little.

Chapter Thirteen

I'm walking down a corridor as wide as the Grand Canyon to reception to see Swain for the show-down and as I'm going past a side-office, I hear my name, so I stopped and this is what I hear.

BAUM: All I'm saying is that he's asked four times when he's going to meet her.

SWAIN: So let him ask.

BAUM: Come on, Harry. You know what I mean.

SWAIN: Yes, certainly. I know what you mean. So let him ask.

BAUM: Harry, the whole thing came out of the fact that the man has been trying to meet Candy We offer him a contract to publicise his story, and of course he accepts because he thinks now he's going to meet her. And if we're honest about it, there was always the promise behind our offer that he <u>would</u> meet her. Now we're getting sensational publicity for Candy, unbelievable publicity, as a matter of fact.

which is helping the film gross and helping her career. And therefore it's helping our percentage and it's helping yours. And we're getting all this for peanuts. Now why can't we be straight with the guy and let him meet her?

SWAIN: I don't care why he accepted the grand, and let's not forget that he <u>does</u> get a grand, for a trigging hospital cleaner . . . .

BAUM: Porter. He's a porter, Harry.

SWAIN: So he's a frigging porter. He still gets a grand. And I don't care what we may or may not have hinted to the guy when we sold him on the idea, as far as I am concerned he gets his money and does what he has to in the contract. and that's it.

BAUM: Harry. What is wrong with Andretti meeting Candy?

SWAIN: Art. Explain to him. He's an old man now and you're young. Explain it to him.

BUCHNER: On balance I still agree with you, Harry, but I just thought we ought to give the whole thing a final airing, but I agree with you, Harry, in the final analysis.

SWAIN: Why do you employ such people, Milton? The boy should be in politics, can't give a straight answer and takes sides with the one who he thinks will advance his career.

BAUM: You still haven't really explained it to me, Harry.

SWAIN: Alright. I'll explain in words of one syllable. This man is a garnicht. A garnicht from garnichtsville. Who is he? What does he know? And who knows what he really is or what he really thinks. Maybe he's just waiting for his chance and wants to stick a knife in Candy. Maybe he wants to strangle her. Who knows? Do you know? I mean can you guarantee he doesn't? Will you give me a written guarantee that he won't harm her? Will you guarantee that there won't be trouble, a scandal, murder, who knows what? You know what these fans are like. And the ones who write and phone and go to the premieres are always the craziest ones. What do you think I am, a charity for crazy people? Supposing he meets her and then sells his story to the Enquirer and tells terrible lies and rumours and kills her career. It's happened. Where is your percentage after that? Percentage of nothing for the sake of a doing the decent thing for crazy man. Let him meet Angelina, She's not our client.

BAUM: Have you asked Candy?

SWAIN: I don't have to ask her, my contract with her says I don't have to, so I don't ask her. She's a sensitive girl, you know. What do you think she wants with a crazy fan around her neck?

BAUM: You don't have to sell her to me, Harry. All I'm saying is, if you haven't asked her, you don't know what she thinks about . . . ."

SWAIN: I don't care what she thinks! I don't have to know what she thinks about this kind of thing I decide this kind of thing and then I tell her. And now I'm telling you. No meeting. No meeting, no sex, no murder. He's had his fun, more than most hospital porters. You know your trouble, Milton . . . .

BAUM: I'm too soft, that's why we've stayed partners for so long.

SWAIN: Exactly.

So now I knew. I was unreliable or I could be unreliable. I was a nut or I could be a nut and who needed it? Not S.o.B. Associates definitely.

I didn't storm in and justify my existence to them. I didn't smash my way through the wall and tell them my pedigree and the pedigree of my ancestors and the pedigree of <u>their</u> ancestors, which was Adolf Hitler and Pol Pot, even though they were Jews. I went home and waited for the end of the week to collect my grand and meanwhile I went on telling the world what a fine person Candy was and I was too.

And I guess I was as far away from Candy as ever, but I put it out of my mind.

Chapter Fourteen

Janet was out, making the world a safer place for decent folk to live in. and I was watching a video-recording of myself on T.V., when the bell rang. It was a young woman, with long, free, brown hair, very thick. She was nearly as tall as me, because she had a pair of red, high-heeled boots on, up to her knees. She had on shorts made of red silk so tight, they showed the shape of her cunt, and cut away at the back so you could see half her rear-end. She had on a skin-tight sweater which stopped just under her breasts and no bra, and she was beautiful in the face with too muchmake-up for my taste. She laughed when she saw me.

"Hello. I've come to get your autograph, Joe."

I said, "Oh, O.K. Wait a second," and I went back inside to get a pen and some paper, which she didn't seem to have. I heard her follow me into the room and close the door. I turned round.

"I don't really want your autograph, Joe. I've come to fuck you, actually."

"That's what you look like, actually." I said, and she laughed her tinkly laugh again. She walked around the room, looking at pictures and a vase of flowers and the T.V.

"I liked your show," she said.

"Thanks."

She turned and stopped in the middle of the room with her hands on her hips and her legs apart. Her tits had hardly moved once.

"Well?" she said, and tinkled again.

"What do you want, get me sacked?"

"I won't tell if you won't."

"How do I know that, kid. They'll stop my contract dead. They'd think I'm a sex maniac or something."

"I was hoping you were, Joe."

"Look, you'd better go. Give me your address and I'll get the agency to send you a photograph. Or you can write in yourself."

"Stop putting me on, Joe. Come on. I'm hot for it. I'm starting to juice. Let's do it. Just make like I'm Candy Starr if you want to."

"What's the matter with you? Do you fuck everything you see on T.V.?"

"Some". She gave me a list of people from the T.V. she'd screwed, including three women.

"What do your parents say about all of this?"

"Jesus Christ! What kind of a phoney are you anyway? What's all the big deal you're putting out on that thing? I wouldn't tell my mother what time of day it was. Come on."

"What do you do?."

"I'm a packer."

"I bet those ain't your working clothes."

"What's the hassle anyway. Not your type, or something. You're so corny, Joe."

"That's right. You're not my type." Who the hell was she anyway. She could be a whore, she could be a kook.

"Let's see."

She lifted her sweater and started to play with her tits. She was rubbing them round slowly and sticking her tongue out of her mouth and flicking it at me. My prick started to grow, which she saw 'cos that's where she was looking.

"Is this your type, Joe?" My prick was growing all the time.

Maybe I'm not your type, Joe, but somebody down there likes me, Joey." She pushed her crutch forward and started rubbing it through the material and still massaging her tits with the other hand and pushing them up at me.

"Is this more your type, Joe?"

She came over and unzipped my flies and started licking my prick. She was all over me, like a crazy young cocker-spaniel our neighbours had, Livorno, the knife-man. She undressed me and used me all over for her pleasure. I hardly did a thing. She just used everything I had and sucked it fucked it and licked it and rubbed it and squeezed it. Her body was like on whole young muscle, and it never stopped moving. I was sighing and moaning, and she must have come half a dozen times. When she was finished, she stood up near my head and looked down at me on the floor through her breasts.

"Is that more your type, Joe?" She was a sweating young peach.

I said, "How did you get my address?"

"No problem," she said.

I felt like saying, "I'm old enough to be your father."

That night I told Janet about her. I didn't say we screwed, but I didn't need to.

"What's the matter with kids like that, she said she wouldn't even tell her own mother what time of day it was?"

"She certainly sounds pretty messed up."

"Yeah, but I'm thinking what you know I'm thinking."

"Are you any different to her, you mean."

"Exactly. She sees me on the screen and wants to screw me just because I'm on there. Before, if she'd seen me in the street, she wouldn't't'uve asked me the time of day either, but just because I go on T.V. and talk about Candy and she seen me in a few magazines also, maybe, or whatever, now she wants my ass."

"I know."

"What do you mean, you know, am I like that really, just because I seen Candy on another screen since I was small, and I want to screw her too, does that make me a mess also?"

Janet thought for a minute.

"I don't think so. For you Candy is some kind of perfect moment to make your life complete, for her, you and the other people she's screwed just mean doing something bad and rebellious to pay back the world or her family or whatever and make them angry, I think it's different."

I looked in the face of this woman who'd stuck by me and loved me and who now was making me feel good because she was intelligent from all her experience of life with the F.B.I. down in the cess-pool, so that she could understand what was going down and explain it and not make me feel I wasn't a jerk like the Sexy Muscle.

"I love you," I said.

God bless Edgar J. Hoover.

Chapter Fifteen

O ne of the T.V. companies offered me a job on a panel for a programme called 'Life Today'. I was the authentic voice from off the street. It paid two grand a week, which I also thought was authentic. I left the hospital, and Mike wished me luck. I gave some money to mama and Janet, and started putting quite a lot away. And I had about ten grand from the agency left from the work for Candy's career. I stayed with them for the new job. Maybe now I getting well-known myself, I'd meet Candy that way after all. Janet left the F.B.I and started looking for something else.

A few months later, Janet got pregnant. I wanted a little girl, but Janet didn't care. I told Janet the kid was gonna be sexy and foul-mouthed and beautiful and lock people up, if they broke the law.

"Sounds O.K.," she said.

I started saving more money.

So what was it?

If you follow the Gospel according to Marinelli, this guy was on a straight road pushing stiffs around a hospital and masturbating and then he leaves his straight road and suddenly everything fucks up. But then that ain't right, exactly, either because on this fucked up road, he meets a good woman who saves him and makes him happy and also he goes back to his first road, but he don't completely leave the road he took when he took the bad turning, so what does that mean?

Hey, you're so fucking clever, you work it out.

Chapter Sixteen

I was asleep

I was on an aeroplane flying to L.A. I couldn't hear the engines. It was like gliding through the white clouds in a dream. I'd eaten the food from the tray and had a couple of drinks, which the stewardess brought me. She had short, blonde hair and a smile to make you feel confident and fly with the airline again next trip. I looked at her legs as she walked down between the seats. So did the guy on the other side of the gangway from me. They was pretty damn good legs and did the airline credit. I was sitting next to a business man type, and we'd talked about Japanese goods coming into the U.S. and if they was as good as ours, which the business man type didn't think they was, of course.

At the airport in L.A., I got into a large, black saloon and we drove to Candy's house. It was summer. The sun was shining and young folk were walking in the streets, pretending that death is only for old people.

When I got to the house, Candy opened the door. She was wearing a light-blue, silk house-coat.

I said, "Hello. My name's Joe Andretti. I've come from New York to make love with you. I've waited a long time."

She smiled, and asked me in. The smile said that she was glad to see me and that she'd been waiting for me. Although, of course, she couldn't have been expecting me, unless the agency did tell her about me. Maybe she saw me on T.V.

We went into a large living-room, which was beautifully set out, with a lot of silk and tasteful colours, like the smart magazines. She gave me a drink and sat down, and her crossed leg showed through the gap in the house-coat.

We talked about why I came and how the journey was, and she was very polite, and didn't act like no big film star at all and then I told her about all my troubles getting to see her and how I'd been crossed up by so many people and how wonderful it was getting to see her at last after such a long, long time and so on and so forth. Then I asked her if it was O.K. if we made love now, and she smiled again very kindly, and came over and sat next to me on the settee.

We made love for a long time, and many times. I can't describe it, but it was everything I always thought it would be. And I knew Candy was very happy with the new turn in her life, 'cos I could feel it.

I remained her lover for many years.

It was a great consolation for the difficulties in my life.

THE END.